KUPWARA
CODES

Praise for *Kupwara Codes*

'Maj Manik Jolly's debut novel, *Kupwara Codes*, is amongst the finest works of military fiction in a long time. Being culled from Indian experiences in counterinsurgency operations, the book gives relevancy to our military literature. Besides, being based on his own service with his Gorkha troops, soldiers par excellence, located in the hottest area of Kashmir insurgency, gives the novel a welcome sense of realism.'

—**Lt Gen Vijay Madan** (Retd.),
ex-Commandant, Army War College, and ex-Colonel of the Regiment, 4 GR

'An action-packed, enthralling novel that immerses you in the world of counterterror operations with remarkable authenticity. The electrifying twists, and the raw, human moments kept me hooked from start to finish. This is military fiction at its finest.'

—**Amish**,
bestselling award-winning author and broadcaster

'Major Jolly's *Kupwara Codes* is an unputdownable thriller, edge-of-the-seat stuff, catches you by the scruff of your neck and does not let go till the last page. A must-read if ever there was one. Can't wait for the next in the series.'

—**Anand Ranganathan**,
author and scientist

'*Kupwara Codes* is a taut counterinsurgency operations thriller and written by a veteran CI Ops practitioner. Read this page-turner for a deep dive into the heart of one of the world's longest running proxy wars.'

—**Sandeep Unnithan**,
author and editor at News9 Plus

'Major Manik's debut novel is military fiction at its finest. His ability to present Army life, operations and interpersonal relations in such an authentic manner is remarkable and riveting. The climax, especially, piques one's excitement and leaves you wanting more.'

—**Aditya Dhar**,
director of the Bollywood blockbuster *Uri*

THE GORKHA GARRISON SERIES
BOOK I

KUPWARA CODES

MAJ MANIK M. JOLLY (RETD)

**HARPER
FICTION**

An Imprint of HarperCollins *Publishers*

First published in India by Harper Fiction 2025
An imprint of HarperCollins *Publishers*
4th Floor, Tower A, Building No. 10, DLF Cyber City,
DLF Phase II, Gurugram, Haryana—122002
www.harpercollins.co.in

2 4 6 8 10 9 7 5 3 1

P-ISBN: 978-93-6213-010-5
E-ISBN: 978-93-6213-347-2

Typeset in 11.5/15 Adobe Garamond at
HarperCollins *Publishers* India

Printed and bound at
Thomson Press (India) Ltd

This book is produced from independently certified FSC® paper
to ensure responsible forest management.

To Maa Saraswati for granting me education and knowledge;

my mother for blessing me with life and wisdom;

and the brave soldiers of the Indian Army, especially from my Gorkha Regiment, for giving me the opportunity to serve and fight for my country

PROLOGUE

LONDON, UNITED KINGDOM

JUNE 2016

The woman scratched the surface of her napkin lightly with a well-manicured nail and absent-mindedly looked out of the window of the posh London restaurant. She didn't speak for a while. General Asim Afridi kept looking at her, waiting for her to speak.

Nobody would have guessed that this kind-faced, fat, bald old man—who looked like someone's grandpa—was responsible for hundreds of bomb blasts and thousands of deaths in India, Afghanistan, Nepal and even Pakistan when required. This was the dreaded Gen Afridi of Pakistan's intelligence organization, ISI. Having retired a few years back, he had settled in London, acting as point-man, negotiator, deal-maker and liaison for the Pakistan Army's nefarious intercations. Today, he was sitting in a fancy restaurant, across from this young woman, who he was informed was a big social media star and podcaster, with millions of followers hanging on to each word she said.

Gen Afridi rarely met low-level operatives and was wondering why the army chief had sent him to meet her. He was used to hanging out with directors and chiefs of foreign agencies who wanted to get things done via or in Pakistan. He was not involved in running active operations anymore, like he used to as the boss of the ISI. So, he was surprised when the chief called and requested him to meet and evaluate her capabilities before the ISI gave a final go-ahead to engage her.

Finally, the woman realized that this man was not the kind you win mind games against. She turned her head towards him and said, 'So what next, General saab?'

He replied calmly, 'You tell me, Sayema. I'm here with a totally open mind, trying to understand your aspirations. If you have cleared the screening and the ISI has arranged this meeting, I'm sure you understand they are already impressed by you. What we need to figure out is if we are sending you to Master Chef, what culinary delights and surprises can be expected from you.'

She smiled lightly, nodded and started speaking passionately. 'You know, General saab, I could've just easily continued my work. I'm a social media star, I am also a communications consultant for celebrities and I earn extremely well. People know me, recognize me and stop to take selfies with me. But then, I asked myself, is that all life is supposed to be? And my heart said "no", I had to answer a bigger call. I had to stand up and do something. I had to give meaning to my existence. That's why I had to contribute to the jihad against India. I am much more capable and enabled than those running around with guns in the jungles of Kashmir. I control minds and narratives. I can help launch revolutions. I can awaken Kashmiris from the slumber they are in and convince them to move against India. You may be judging me when I say all this because all you see is a modern "pretty young thing". But trust me, General saab, the hate I carry in my heart is not only an exceptional motivator, but also gives me direction. I am actually very thankful to the ISI for contacting me and giving me this chance. In the last few months, I have been thinking hard about what I can do best. All I need now is a green signal and details on when and how.'

She leaned back in her chair and looked straight into Gen Afridi's eyes. Sayema Haider was a famous YouTuber from London, who after having achieved a lot in the material world suddenly felt the need to attend to her religious calling. Slowly and steadily, she moved up in this world too, dropping hints at various forums that she was ready to do more. The listening walls took the message to the ISI, and finally, she got her attendance with the scheming old fox of ISI, Afridi.

He nodded lightly and, placing his elbows on the table, said softly while leaning ahead, 'Sayema, the hate that you carry for India is not new to us. Every Pakistani hates India with equal passion. But if GHQ has chosen to work with you, I am sure they have their reasons. I am here just to see if you are keen to work with us, and how we can utilize you. So, tell me, what's making you jump on this ship? The Pakistani Army, and I personally, will make sure that you get full support.'

He gave a little smile. Decades of groundwork had taught Afridi never to make the first offer.

'I don't know, sir. How would you like me to proceed?' Sayema asked.

Afridi had her exactly where he wanted, itching for action.

'Well, Sayema, from now on, let this hate not dictate your actions. It's crippling and blinding. What I am about to tell you, and what you will be doing for the next few years, requires a very stable, clear and balanced mind. Think big! We are very selective about the people we work with. We know that illiterate and jobless young guys are good enough only to run around in jungles with guns. They are created just to keep the Indian Army occupied and irritated. You are much smarter and more competent. What we can do together will be phenomenal. We will create chaos, the kind India has never seen before. We will create a state of anarchy where everyone in the Valley will rise with guns in their hands and decimate the Indian Army. We will usher in a revolution to free Kashmir. What do you say?'

Afridi finished his monologue that came with his best acting skills, animated hand gestures and a piercing stare that never left Sayema.

Her face was flushed with excitement. Afridi's words had done the magic—he was the guru of motivating young people to march happily to their deaths. He must have said these words millions of times—to young terrorists, to suicide bombers, to anarchists, to Kashmiri separatists, or anyone who volunteered to harm India.

'General saab, I am honoured that you think so highly of me. Whatever you need, please let me know. I am at your service,' said Sayema, barely able to speak with all the excitement.

'Hope you know enough about Kashmir?' he asked.

Suddenly, her face hardened. With a scowl, she said, 'What can I say? On the night of 12 May 1994, the Indian Army carried out an operation in Baramulla, where two civilians were also killed. One of them was my father. I was only nine years old. My uncle took my mother and me to London, and we settled here. Now, we are British citizens. But since that night, the only thing that matters to me is revenge—for me, my family and all Kashmiris. So yes, I know Kashmir. And I would be surprised if you didn't know this already.'

Afridi smiled. Of course, he knew all this. He also knew this was the story she told everyone to position herself as some righteous flagbearer of justice. Whereas the reality was that her father was a terror financier, who was killed by local Kashmiri terrorists when he was caught embezzling. But there was no point contradicting her. People need dreams and fantasies to keep themselves motivated, so let her have hers.

Sayema, of course, had no idea that he knew this. But he always did his homework, and what he knew best was how to take a subject to their emotional peak, and then use that adrenalin-ridden state to convince them to do whatever he wanted them to.

He really liked what he saw—potential, motivation, cover and aggression. The file was not lying. The only thing he had to figure out was how to use this unique gem and get the most out of her.

He took off his glasses and placed them on the table. Looking into her eyes with a near-hypnotizing gaze, he said, 'Till the day there are fighters like you in this world, nobody can stop the independence of Kashmir. I am going to talk to Gen Gaffur. Give me some time to get back to you with a plan. Meanwhile, I hope you understand that this meeting never happened.'

Sayema let out a hearty laugh and said, 'General saab, if I didn't know this much, this meeting definitely wouldn't have happened.'

They both laughed, raised their wine glasses and nodded to each other in a mock salute. Afridi took a small sip, kept the glass back down and said, seriously, 'Do you know that the chief minister's office in Kashmir is looking for a media consultant?'

1

KUPWARA, KASHMIR, INDIA

JULY 2017

They slowly moved the leaves in front of them aside and, looked ahead, at the little glimmer in the dense jungle below them on the ridge line, trying hard to focus in the dying light of the day. The quick dance of light and shadows was too fickle to make out any shapes, but there was a tiny glow, like a large firefly in the far distance, and that meant only one thing—a terrorist who could not resist smoking while hiding in the bushes.

Danny turned his head towards Deepak, tapped him on the shoulder and asked, 'So? Ready for action, D-Cup?'

Deepak nodded in a dazed state and barely let out a 'Yes, sir'.

'Good. Now, we wait till dark and then move forward. You go around three hundred metres up and block them from the top. I'll send another stop party down, and we box them in. Be alert and play safe. You see someone coming from the top or the sides towards these guys, let him go. That way, you will guide him into your box. Don't fire at those guys, got it?'

Danny thought repeating the plan would ensure the youngster, in his exuberance, didn't forget the basics.

'Got it, sir. But what if no one comes towards us? I'll not get to kill anyone,' said Deepak.

'Buddy, even though you have been christened "D-Cup", try your best not to act and talk like a real fucking boob, okay? Go and man your stop. Do not fire unless someone is firing at you, or I ask you to. And don't get killed. I don't know your parents, so it'll be really uncomfortable meeting them for the first time with your ashes. Spare me that agony!'

All the while he was talking, Danny kept checking his equipment.

'But it's a privilege and honour to die for the country, sir,' Deepak whispered proudly.

Danny took out a cigarette pack from his pocket, opened it, took out one stick, took a long whiff along its length, kept it back in and closed the box. He looked at Deepak straight in the eye and said, 'Listen, junior. Let's get off the philosophical high horse. I didn't join the Army to use this privilege and honour. I joined it to ensure the enemy uses his. That should be your guiding beacon of military philosophy. Let him die for his country; I'm not interested. It'll serve you well throughout your career.' He kept the packet back in his pocket.

Maj Danny Deka was about to show his one-month-old company officer why he was known as the 'Hunter of Kupwara'.

2

Deepak took almost an hour to reach the designated location. Although it was just a few hundred metres away, moving with stealth in a dense jungle at night is always very slow and deliberate. Once there, he knew very well that this was the first time his troops would see him in an active operation. In a way, he considered himself very lucky that within a month of joining, he was about to see some action. People spend decades in the army without experiencing combat. Aside from the stories they tell back home, only a handful in the entire Army can boast about being in active combat. Being with Danny and his unit, Deepak learnt pretty quickly that the ones who dispatch the terrorists to the 'heavenly virgins' rarely talk, and the ones who are combat virgins can't shut up about their made-up exploits.

Deepak also knew well that your conduct during operations can make or break your image in the unit. He must have heard the story of the young officer who panicked and hid behind a fallen tree during an entire gunfight a million times. Troops narrated that story with a lot of laughter and thigh-slapping at every party, much to the embarrassment of other officers. He did not want to be 'that guy'. The fact that this particular officer went on to become a brigadier and would be a general one day is another story altogether. Still, Deepak wanted his troops to respect him the way they respected Maj Danny.

Lieutenant Deepak Lathwal was not from a military background. His parents were both teachers in Rohtak, Haryana, but he had dreamt about being an army officer for as long as he could remember. He cleared his NDA entrance on his first go, and four years later, he opted to join one of the finest battalions in the Indian Army, the First Battalion of Fourth Gorkha Rifles, commonly known as First Four. He knew life would be tough. He knew days would be long and nights dangerous. He knew there would be no respite from endless patrolling and ambushes. What he didn't know was that he would find himself serving under the most famous Major of the Northern Command, and that the bar would be set so high. After all, Deepak wanted to be the hero of his first movie, not a sidekick to an Amitabh Bachchan. For what it was worth, he hoped he would come out of this having learnt a lot, and become an excellent field operative and troop commander.

He sat down and scanned the area again. There was hardly any visibility, but he knew where he was. The terrorists were around 250 metres below him, at the middle of the spur. He had been instructed to block their way from above to ensure they couldn't escape once the firing started. Who runs up the mountain? Well, the terrorists who know the Army's tactics well and are familiar with stop parties on the downward path do. They run upwards and vanish into the jungle. Not that it was a great insight, but the fact that he hadn't known this made him realize how much he still had to learn. Life was very different from what academies taught you, or what the blabber from social media experts revealed.

Deepak knew his troops had been in many operations, and would judge every decision he took, even though they would follow it unquestioningly. He asked the LMG squad to be at the highest point so they could get a clean sweep of the entire area. He placed a few more guys in batches of two behind a few trees, and took position in the middle with his radio operator behind another tree. He was happy with the crescent shape he had created with his team, covering a large enough area for both observation and firing. Now, the wait began. He wondered if Danny would finish them all off on his own, or would his action send one scurrying along his way? If someone did come, would he be able to shoot him, or would one of his guys take out the bad guy before he had a chance to do something? Tomorrow morning, when the Sitrep was sent, would it feature his name, or would he just be part of the 'party of forty-five soldiers' that went into the operation? So many questions, so many aspirations, so many doubts. And only one man could make his dreams come true—the terrorist who decided to run up the hill.

'Oh God, please make someone run up the hill. Please. I will offer twenty-five kilos of laddoos in the temple. Just send me one guy,' he prayed desperately.

A tap on his shoulder pulled him out of his bargaining with the almighty. His radio operator shoved the handset in his hand and mumbled, 'Tiger'. He took the handset urgently and whispered, 'D-Cup for Tiger, over.'

Deepak hated his code name.

'You in position? Over,' Danny asked.

'Yes, sir. Over,' Deepak said crisply.

'Good. Stay sharp. Diwali in the next ten minutes. Over and out.'

Danny never wasted any breath or word. His chain-smoking had given him a baritone, which is actually very bad for radio communication since most words sounded a little garbled because of the deep and heavy voice. Thankfully, this wasn't a long conversation. All Deepak had to do was to move the safety catch of his AK to 'fire' and signal to those around him to do the same. Everyone could see the next guy, so the message was complied with within seconds. The Gorkhas were ready, Deepak was ready, their rifles were ready. But where was the target?

3

Danny had also sent a second party to block the path going down from the terrorists' hideout. He planned to attack them from the front with his party, and hoped that anyone running up or down the spur would be caught by the other two parties. On the other side of the spur was a steep cliff of around a hundred feet, so it was fair to assume that no one would jump to his death, and would run up or down the spur only.

Danny had received intelligence that there were five terrorists in the hideout, and the little movement he could notice—a flicker of light now and then—confirmed it. All he wanted was to kill them quickly and have a smoke. The moment you enter the jungle, you cannot smoke—it can be smelled and its glow can be seen hundreds of metres away. So Danny kept sniffing his cigarettes to manage his craving for the time being.

Once he was sure the two other parties were in position, he signalled to his own team to move out. Tonight was going to be a long night, Danny knew. He had left the company base the moment he had received the intelligence, but the rest of the companies from his unit would not be able to join before noon the next day, due to the distances and climbs involved. Generally, the CO would have preferred this to be a two-company or even three-company operation. But there was no time; terrorists don't linger around the same location for long.

If only Danny had a penny for every time he had climbed a mountain and found nothing there, he could've bought his dream car by now.

Even though he loved the organization and his unit more than his life, he disliked a lot of things about the Army—the bureaucracy, the sycophancy, the zero-error syndrome and, especially, the indecisive top brass. He was loved by his troops as a fearless officer and an exceptionally good combat leader. He did not have a problem with authority, a popular notion among his seniors, but with autocracy. The tiny gap between the two is where wisdom and leadership resided.

Danny checked his khukri, AK, pistol and grenades and started walking slowly towards the destination. For such operations, he always wore the clothes of the terrorists he had killed, because of a superstitious belief that someone was supposed to die in these clothes, and as someone had died already he had a higher chance of surviving. After operations, he was often greeted by his CO with a 'what the fuck are you wearing?'. But Danny placed more faith in this belief than his boss's conformist ideology. He would later apologize for being wrongly dressed, the CO would grunt and, then, everyone would move on. It was always the same drill. The fact that the CO was very fond of him gave him some leverage to play around with some rules that he loved breaking.

He knew that the same discussion awaited the next morning. But now was not the time to worry about it. He needed all his focus on the task at hand. Nothing mattered to him more than killing as many terrorists as possible. Somehow, this 'hunting in the dark' was the only place where he truly shone. This was his zone, his territory, and his expertise. He never wanted to believe that these drug-addled, barely trained and wrongly motivated terrorists could outwit him at this game. He always entered the jungle with just one worry—'hope I don't miss killing anyone from the group'. His mind worked at full throttle, his senses were enhanced, and somehow, he developed a broader vision whenever he took those steps in the thick undergrowth. He was a true hunter, in every sense of the word.

Danny reached his designated location right before the break of dawn. The terrorists were just a hundred metres away, but still not visible. He needed a better vantage point to fire effectively, and was worried they might vanish soon, so there was no time to lose. He quickly signalled the spots he wanted his team to position themselves.

He believed in running them down, and not gunning them down in the first go. He often had arguments with his CO on this tactical take. However, the success of his operations proved that it was a solid strategy. He would fire as much as possible into the group or hideout and make them run towards his boys. A running and scared enemy is much easier to take a clean shot at by a well-placed soldier than trying to get them all in one go and forcing them to fight back. And thus, his strategy was to fire just enough to make them believe they had a chance to get away and decide to run. And then welcome them to the jaws of Delta company's ferocious Gorkhas!

The intelligence had come from a local farmer who had gone to collect mushrooms in the jungle and seen these terrorists. He had immediately informed Danny about it. Such information was as rare as it was dangerous. Danny could very well walk his team into a trap. But that's the risk he and thousands of soldiers of the Indian Army had to take every day. Danny had developed an excellent intelligence network, mainly due to his personal dealings with people from neighbouring villages.

Even the villagers, who had seen nearly three decades of Army deployment, understood the officers very well—they knew who was a politician just paying lip service but not taking action; who was a career soldier passing time to get done with his field tenure; and who was a real daredevil, with nothing but the annihilation of terrorists on his mind. They appreciated Danny's no-nonsense approach. When he said he was there to protect them, he really meant it. And in turn, the villagers did their best to protect the soldiers by giving them whatever information they could.

Danny moved around and found a good spot from where he had a clear view of the hideout. He saw two terrorists eating something from a can, and one just casually packing a rucksack and a sleeping bag. He observed them for a while and did not see anyone else. But the farmer had told him there were five. Take on these three and risk losing others as they might vanish? Wait to confirm all five? Take on these three and hope the other two were caught by the parties on the top and bottom of the spur? Time was ticking, and Danny was running the options through his mind. Finally, he decided that three dead terrorists were better than none, and signalled to his team to get ready to fire.

The first impact needed to shake the terrorists to the core, so the party needed to fill the area with as much lead as possible.

But even before he could touch his trigger, Danny heard the unmistakable burst of AK firing. And then some more. It came from the direction of the base of the spur.

Suddenly, the whole jungle was filled with the deafening and continuous bursts of AK rifles engaging in loud firing. In the split second that he was distracted, Danny saw from the corner of his eye that the three guys he had locked on to had stood up and run off at lightning speed. In a second, his entire plan fell apart—he had no one to fire upon. All he knew was that they had run towards the top of the spur, where Deepak's team was placed. What was happening with the team at the bottom, he had no idea. And he was not going to call and badger them with questions. Whatever had to happen would happen in the next sixty seconds and he wanted his team to focus on firing and not get disturbed by his call.

Yet, he looked at his radio guy and said, 'Deepak'.

'That,' he thought in his mind, 'ladies and gentlemen is the crux of CI operations. You can plan and plan and plan for every contingency, and still the jungle will surprise you with the unthinkable.'

4

Deepak also heard the firing and, immediately, his whole body tensed. He had never heard gunfire in real life. All he had done was train at the academy firing range. This sounded different—there was a certain unruliness and arrogance to it. It wasn't disciplined firing by cadets lying or standing in firing positions, aiming at that figure a few hundred feet away, where you could expect the cacophony to pierce your ears periodically. This was savage and scary.

He looked around and saw everyone tighten their grip on their rifles and point them at the area in front. His hope to kill the terrorists quickly turned into a subconscious need to survive and not get shot. He wished someone could tell him what was happening.

As if on cue, Deepak got a call from Danny.

'D-Cup, they are coming your way. Take control. I am coming as quickly as I can. Over and out.'

They? More than one? Deepak's legs were shaking a little bit now.

Will they come straight at me? One by one or all together? How many bullets does it take to kill someone? Hope we don't crossfire into each other … Can they run over us? Could we end up with casualties? His mind was racing at lightning speed, and he did not want to look towards his boys, fearing they might see him panicking. He realized he was gripping the handset so tight that his knuckles had turned white. That's when he saw the radio operator looking at him calmly.

The operator took the handset from him and said something Deepak knew would stay with him for the rest of his life, 'Sir, just look through the sight and press the trigger, shouting "Jai Mahakali" when you see them. There is nothing more to it.'

Hearing this unconventional wisdom relaxed Deepak a bit, and he looked into the forest in front of him. Nothing happened for a few minutes; even the firing stopped. His radio guy chimed in again, 'Sir, the stop at the base got two guys. Everyone's safe on our side. Tiger said three are coming our way.'

'So this is it,' Deepak thought. 'There are three running towards us. They will appear any moment from the bushes in front, and we hardly have twenty feet of clearing between us and the bushes. Whatever happens will happen in these twenty feet. Two seconds at most. A moving target is never easy, and a moving target that fires back at you is definitely not easy. Should I tap them one by one, two shots on each, and move to the next? Or should I just empty a magazine into the crowd? I just don't want them crossing the clearing alive. Maybe if…'

And exactly then, a man appeared from the bushes huffing and puffing, wearing a loose combat jacket over a combat shirt and pants, with an AK in his hands. His flowing beard seemed to move in slow motion. In a fraction of a second, he saw Deepak in front of him; before that second was over, he had lowered his rifle and was trying to aim when Deepak pressed the trigger with all the strength he had. He did not aim much; it was as if he believed that his rifle would follow his line of sight automatically. But he did not let go of the trigger until he heard a loud click, indicating that the magazine was empty. Suddenly, he felt lost and dazed. He didn't even remember he had a few more magazines.

The whole place was now filled with loud cracks of gunfire and shouting. He could hardly discern who was saying what. He squinted through the smoke and dust and saw not one but two men lying in front, motionless and at awkward angles. It took him a moment to gather himself and snap back from the stupor to realize that they had killed two of them. He looked at his radio operator and found him all red-faced—cheerful, excited and nodding vigorously. 'Yes, sir, yes, we did it.'

'But there were three,' Deepak said, suddenly remembering. 'Maybe the third is hiding in the bushes. He did not reach the clearing.'

Deepak shouted to his team at the top of his voice, 'Stay where you are and stay alert. There is one more.'

He was in control now. He had done it. He had delivered. Now he just had to wait and get the third one, and they could go home safe and happy. He was not going to let the third idiot ruin his day. Patience, he kept telling himself.

On the other side, Danny was climbing the hill as fast as he could, his lungs screaming for air, knees asking for a new lease of life. He was pushing his body to its limit trying to reach Deepak. For Danny, every soldier under his command was like his family—he just could not sit and wait for things to unfold.

Then, he heard the bursts of fire. He dived straight to the ground and covered his head with his arms. A couple of seconds passed, and Danny realized that the firing was around fifty metres in front and above him. He knew what was happening, but he also knew that any possibility of him going up was now closed, as he would be walking directly into Deepak's team's bullets. 'Lucky bastard! Getting a kill on his first operation. I hope he's okay,' Danny thought to himself, and immediately took cover behind a fallen tree.

If Deepak had killed all of them, he would know within a few minutes. If he had not been able to, he would know in the next few seconds, because any survivor would be running down frantically and coming straight towards him. He asked his team to take position quickly and scan the area above them for any movement. He muttered 'Jai Mahakali' softly and looked at his radio operator, who showed a determined face and whispered back, 'Ayo Gorkhali.'

Danny had not even finished sitting down properly when he heard loud rustles in the bushes ahead. The thick undergrowth had no clearing; he wouldn't even know who was there unless that person was within ten feet of him. And in that small space, it would just be a matter of who press the trigger first. Danny brought his rifle to his shoulder, peered down the sights with his finger on the trigger, sank to one knee and took a long breath. He may not have known a lot about many things, but he surely knew how to punch holes in fleeing terrorists.

The noise gave way to a quick glimpse of a black jacket moving in the thicket, undoubtedly coming directly towards him. Danny started counting. It was a trick he had learnt long ago and taught his team. Just before the climax, count. It somehow takes away the stress and keeps you focused.

'One, two…'

He felt the cold steel of the trigger and wrapped his finger around it.

'Three, four…'

He pushed the AK back onto his shoulder.

'Five, six…'

He looked into the bushes above the sights to get a better view as he knew the black jacket was almost there.

'Seven…'

He saw the black jacket emerge from the bushes, got him in his sights and pressed the trigger.

'Eight…'

Danny let out a long breath and his body relaxed.

The black jacket and the body hosting the garment had two holes in the chest now. Blood seeping through the clothes and a surprised look on the terrorist's face was all that was left there.

Danny looked at his radio operator and asked him to check Deepak's status, and if they could come up. His job for the day was done, and it was not even breakfast time yet.

Deepak heard a neat, sharp two-round burst. Apparently, like breath and words, Danny didn't waste ammunition either—he got the fifth terrorist in the middle of the spur when this guy backed up from Deepak's position and was trying to vanish into the jungle.

Deepak's radio guy looked at him and, smiling from ear to ear, said, 'Tiger's style. Tap, tap, tap!'

And then there were five!

5

Danny and Deepak got called to the unit HQ the next day. It was around a two-hour walk from the company location to the road, and then a treacherous three-hour drive down winding mountain roads. Whenever Danny moved, he always took his Ghatak platoon with him, which also served as his QRT. Normally all Infantry units have one Ghatak platoon as per organization. But Danny's unit has created one for each company, equipped them ideally and created some additional lethal teams.

He was planning to train Deepak as the company's Ghatak commander. It was not so much about physical fitness, he always told his team, as it was about mental toughness. 'Even a mule is fitter than us,' he used to say. That's why he spent a lot of time training his boys on how to become ultimate warriors—fearless, constantly aware of the changing situation in any encounter and lethal sharpshooters.

Danny was a leader of a different kind. He spent most of his time with his men, trying to understand them individually. His message to Deepak the day he joined the company had been, 'It is only when we know who is good for what that we

24

can position the right soldier at the right place with the right weapon and the right target.'

Danny Deka came from a lower-middle-class family in Majuli, one of the largest river islands in the world, which stands in the middle of the Brahmaputra River. He had spent his childhood learning to run, swim and survive the floods.

Right from boyhood, Danny had been a bit more mature, silent and tough than the regular kids. He wanted to get out from the shackles of that island, where the limits ended once the waters started, and see the world. He wanted a life of action and adventure. His family was extremely patriotic, and the zeal to join the Army was present in him right from childhood. His older sister graduated from Guwahati University and married an ONGC engineer; Danny visited them whenever he was on leave, and his little nephew and toddler niece—whom he called 'Grenade One' and 'Grenade Two'—were now his favourite people in the world.

Danny rarely spoke about his military life at home or with friends. In fact, his reserved nature extended to him enjoying his solitude both while on duty and on leave. He would sit for hours staring at the waters of the Brahmaputra River at home, or the snow-clad mountains when on duty. But his mind was like a hot wire, never resting. He read, read and read, even when he had five minutes free. He truly believed that he was not meant to become a general, but he wanted to be the best at what he did as a company commander. So, moments of physical inaction and rest were the most turbulent in his mind—he kept going over the intel and details he had about the terrorists operating in an area.

Because he read extensively and never missed a chance to talk to someone who he thought could teach him a thing or two, he was always willing to learn and he could talk about any topic or subject under the sun. Nor did he ever shy away from speaking when he felt he had to give his input, without caring who was present. For him, the greatest cowardice was in keeping quiet when you are supposed to talk. He definitely practised what he preached and that ensured he wasn't invited to many conferences, parties or interactions.

Danny and Deepak left their base early in the morning and walked through the ups and downs of the terrain, crossed a small stream and reached the road just before 10 a.m. The team mounted the vehicles and Danny took the driver's seat asking Deepak to sit next to him. 'When your senior is driving a Jeep or a Gypsy, wait for him to tell you to sit as co-driver. Don't assume. He may ask you to sit behind too, for any reason. Point being, wait for instructions.'

'Thank you, sir, noted,' said Deepak, taking his seat. 'What if you are driving a truck, sir?'

Danny was just letting the Gypsy roll forward when he suddenly applied the brake. As the vehicle came to a halt, he looked at Deepak and said, 'Get this tattooed on your thick skull, I don't drive trucks. Now get down, go and sit as the co-driver in the truck behind. Ask the driver all the transport-related questions you have.'

Deepak apologized, got down, ran to the 2.5-tonner following Danny's Gypsy. Rather than climbing into the cabin, he went back and joined the troops in the rear. As soon as he raised his arm, a smiling Gorkha pulled him up into the truck. All the boys smiled at each other, knowing full well that the new officer was undergoing training. Danny was ruthless in training and had little patience for nonsense. He never pampered anyone; rather, he believed in teaching lessons that would never be forgotten. Although he sent Deepak to the truck to give the impression of disciplining him, Danny knew that travelling with the troops would give Deepak more chances to introduce himself, interact with them and get to know them better in a more informal manner here. If young officers do not spend enough time with their troops, and stay cocooned in their ivory towers, the bonds crucial for managing a team are not formed.

In the truck, Deepak was already practising his Nepali with the boys, eating the Gorkhali snacks they were carrying and drinking the infamous 'jam-paani'—a concoction made by mixing jam with boiling water. Soldiers liked to know about their young leaders, so they always asked questions about their hometowns, families and education. The younger, cheekier ones even asked about girlfriends. It was more than a family, where bonds were built with faith and perseverance.

The CHM Vishnu Prasad Thapa handed Deepak some pakodas and asked, 'Is your father also in the Army, sir?'

Deepak shook his head and said, 'No, Dai ("brother" in Nepali). Both my parents are teachers. I am from Rohtak, Haryana, famous for wrestlers, soldiers and daring people. Some day, I will take you all there and we can go to this famous hangout called D Park, and I will treat you to the best samosas and gulab jamuns in the world. You will forget the shit they sell here!'

The troops laughed, and someone started correcting the Nepali Deepak had just spoken. It was the duty of the company boys to teach their officers the language, and everyone took it seriously.

Decades pass and lives change, but for infantry officers, these unfiltered, heart-to-heart conversations were the ones that became the milestones in the memories of their military careers. Those old and frail men are now walking with sticks and trying hard to press tiny buttons on new mobile phones. But when they closed their eyes and remembered the days when they were vibrant, young and dashing leaders of men, they often paused at these interactions to relive them again in their minds and smile peacefully with the satisfaction of a life fully lived. There was nothing more to it—just the bonds that you made, the men you lost and the memories you carried.

6

Colonel Abhishek Deo was on the phone when he waved Danny and Deepak inside his office and signalled to them to sit down. The call went on for another couple of minutes and the duo kept looking at the various maps and trophies displayed in the office.

Their CO had a huge teakwood table and a comfortable leather chair. The flags of India and the 4th Gorkha Rifles were placed behind him on either side. The large window behind him had a great view of the entire camp and the mountains behind it. Photographs of previous commanding officers—the 'Rogues' Gallery' as it was called—were placed on a wooden shelf which ran along three walls in a line.

Once Deo hung up, he took a file from his drawer, placed it open in front of them and asked, 'You know what this is, right?'

'Yes, sir. It's the list of OGWs in the AOR,' Danny replied. Then turning to Deepak, he said, 'That's over-ground workers and area of responsibility.'

Deepak nodded. He really didn't want to appear like a novice in front of the CO and make a bad impression. He felt comfortable knowing Danny had his back, and would ensure he was not left out of the conversation and explain things that Deepak did not understand.

'So, a few of them fall in your AOR,' Col Deo began. 'I need you to keep an eye on them and maintain an observation log. This operation indicates these guys are moving through the area, so let us start investigating seriously. Send a fortnightly report of your special observations to the adjutant. Let's stay sharp.'

'Noted, sir. Any of them we should focus more on?' Danny asked.

'Nothing specific came in from Brigade HQ. I'll check again and get back to you. But it is actually up to you to generate intelligence and send it to me, so I can send it to HQ. They just collate and share; you are the man on the ground. So, honestly, people up the chain depend on you to surveil these OGWs,' he said, emphasizing his last line.

'Understood, sir,' Danny replied. 'We will get on with it and send regular reports. Anything else for us, sir?'

'Nothing as of now. The real reason I called you here is that tomorrow, we have to go to Srinagar to meet the corps commander. He always likes to meet the team commanders who carry out operations. We leave early in the morning. For now, let me finish some work here, and then we'll have some beer in the Mess.'

The CO smiled and leaned back in his chair, waiting for them to get up and leave.

Danny said, 'Yes, sir.'

As he was getting up to leave, Deepak asked, 'Sir, how do we decide who is an OGW? In some cases, entire villages in our AOR support the terrorists when they are passing by. Are they all OGWs?'

The CO and Danny looked at each other, then at Deepak, and then at each other again. Danny sat down and asked the CO, 'Sir, you'll take this, or should I?'

The CO nodded at Danny to go ahead, still leaning back in his chair.

Danny turned his chair towards Deepak, cracked his knuckles and said, 'Deepak, it is very important for you to understand whom you are fighting here. Our mental biases, lack of perception and immature gossip lead to the creation of a wrong image of the entire thing. You have to be clear about who is who. Just because you have the gun doesn't mean everyone is a target.'

He paused and looked at the CO, who gave a satisfied nod.

'Everyone you will ever meet in Kashmir falls in some category, and you should know how to deal with it,' Danny continued. 'It's a whole spectrum and you need to be very sorted in terms of handling each colour. Let's say the first lot are the regular people, worried about their lives and property, struggling with their daily challenges. They think of themselves as true Indians. These people may have minimal to no information on things that could be of use to us, but they do not want to associate with either the Army or the extremists. Their biggest gripe is when they are coloured in the same shade as others who engage in separatism and insurgency. So, make it a rule to never trouble people unnecessarily—it not only impedes your judgement about finding the real targets, but also brings a bad name to the Army.'

The CO, who was listening keenly to Danny, started writing something in his notepad. When Danny looked at him, he smiled and said, 'That's a great way to explain, Danny. Crisp and clear. I'm going to use these points when I brief the youngsters.'

Danny smiled back and replied, 'Thanks, sir. Just sharing my observations.'

Then, he turned to Deepak again and continued, 'Then come the sympathizers. This is the lot that hates us, especially the Indian Army, and sympathizes with the terrorists and separatists. Their loyalties do not lie with India, and they live in this delusion that the financially and morally bankrupt Pakistan is their saviour. They come out in protest and wreak havoc on social media with their propaganda, and some of them are also part of sleeper cells. From time to time, a few will support terrorists with basic logistical support or information on security forces. These are the most dangerous people, in a way, because there are hundreds of thousands of them, and they are everywhere. It is impossible to find and track them and, hence, they are somehow the core reason for the entire chaos in the Valley. If you can take away these guys, the backbone of terrorism will snap, and it'll be a matter of days before Kashmir is safe and normal again.'

'How do we identify them?' Deepak asked.

Danny shook his head. 'We can't. And even if you do, you really cannot do much against someone who just has an opinion and a choice different from yours. You have to wait for them to do something that can lead to an arrest. And that, again, is not possible with such a large population,' he explained.

Deepak was taking notes diligently. At this point he looked up and asked, 'How do we deal with them?'

This time, it was the CO who replied. 'Deepak, the armed forces technically have a limited role to play here. It is a political game, and the onus is upon the government to ensure that the Kashmiris feel part of India. The Army is simply an executive branch that acts upon the government's orders. They say "go and fight a war", and we do it. They say "go and deploy in Kashmir", and we do. One day, they might say "come back", and we will. However, we are here to do the specific task of uprooting terrorism and killing terrorists. In that, there are no compromises. Whatever needs to be done to achieve that goal, we should do it and stay focused.

'The problem comes when we try and become politicians, and politicians start to become generals. When you are out there, always remember you are operating in your own country, among your own citizens, and it is only the terror elements your gun should be pointed at. Never hurt a citizen, never let bias cloud your judgement, never be scared to carry out your duties. We are part of a ruthless and violent machine that should invoke fear in the hearts—of our enemies. That is our primary duty,' he finished.

'Right, sir,' said Deepak.

'And then come the OGWs. The over-ground workers are identified supporters of terrorism and separatism. These are people who have, at one time or the other, been involved actively in such activities. All these people lead normal lives and are part of the local crowd, but they harbour a deep resentment towards India and the Army, and secretly keep helping our enemies. Some of them may not engage in these activities constantly, but it is advisable to keep an eye on them because they are the support system that enables the movement and operation of terrorists from across and beyond the border and within the Valley and, sometimes, even the rest of the country. Their perfect civilian cover gives them adequate leverage to help them carry out these tasks without being caught,' Danny explained the next part.

Deepak looked up from his notes and asked, 'Why aren't they arrested?'

The CO spoke again. 'Well, it is not that easy. Some of them have finished their sentences in jail, some got clemency as they are surrendered terrorists, some got out early because of political patronage, etc.,' he said. 'The point is, they are where they are due to the government's decision to give them a second chance to have a normal life. But it is highly doubtful that their opinions have changed, so we keep an eye on them. As of now, they are not actively engaged in anything which we can arrest them for. It is not possible to act against anyone just on gut feeling or past record. But what is possible is to keep them under surveillance—sometimes secretly, sometimes even showing them they are under our watchful eye. That acts as a deterrent. Nothing is sacrosanct. As field commander, you will have to take these calls. Also, some of them have just never been caught or even identified. Those guys have been helping Pakistan's cause for decades, but have never stepped into the limelight.'

Deepak nodded vigorously. He was feeling like the entire load of Kashmir was somehow being put on his shoulders—a feeling that all young officers got when they were introduced to the realities of counterterrorism operations. But slowly, they would realize that despite so many possibilities, data and information, it might be years before they even got to fire at a terrorist. In some cases, it may never happen. Finding a needle in a haystack was easier than finding a terrorist hiding within thousands of square kilometres of jungles and mountains in Kashmir.

He looked at Danny and said, 'The only category left must be the terrorists now?'

Danny smiled, looked at the CO and remarked, 'We have a smart one here, sir.' They both laughed.

'Yes, then there are terrorists,' Danny continued. 'But how you approach them also depends on their categories. There are lads who want to become terrorists—we call them "aspirants". Then, there are local terrorists operating here, and local guys in training camps in Pakistan. Some are Pakistani terrorists; some are even from Afghanistan. These are more like contract killers—they are here to carry out acts of terror for some time and then go back. The locals, however, will stay longer. There are also surrendered terrorists, who pick up guns again. There are trainers, guides, funders and others, who are experts at their skills. There are those who never pick up guns here, but go out of Kashmir to carry out acts of terror. And then there are fidayeens, the suicide bombers.'

Danny took a pause and looked intently at Deepak. 'All these types have different styles of operating, separate intelligence channels and tasks. You will have to sift through all the intelligence and figure out who you are dealing with, and then act appropriately. If you thought this would be like a video game where all the enemies would be marked in red on the map, you're wrong. We operate in a very complicated landscape, and while a hundred of your actions can go unnoticed and unrewarded, one wrong action can either lead to mass casualties for us, or even finish your career. Read all the inputs regularly, stay alert and be a thinking commander,' he said, and straightening his chair to face the CO again announced silently that he had said his piece.

The CO waved in the air and added, 'And then there is the media, the humanitarian organizations and the think-tanks. We will get to them some other day.'

Deo let out a chuckle, and Danny and Deepak stood up and saluted crisply. The CO looked at both of them and said, 'See you guys in the Mess. Also, I'll stay with one of my coursemates in Srinagar at Corps HQ. Both of you tie up at the Transit camp in Srinagar if you want to stay. It's your choice if you want to come back.'

'Yes, sir,' they both replied as Deo walked out of his office with them.

7

Lieutenant General Kshitij Balhara sat reading a file behind his large walnut desk. The office was adorned with photographs of previous corps commanders, and many beautiful plaques and mementoes were hung on the walls and placed aesthetically around the room on small tables and in curio cabinets. Behind his chair stood exquisitely embroidered flags representing the 15 Corps, the Northern Command and the Army, as well as the national flag.

The room was spacious, with huge windows on one side overlooking the cantonment. The wooden walls had a teak finish. There were two very comfortable-looking leather chairs opposite where Balhara sat, and a large sofa, two sofa chairs and a table in one corner of the room. Tastefully arranged plants gave a very lively feel to the room, even amid all the wood and leather.

Col Deo, Maj Danny and Lt Deepak entered Balhara's room along with Brigadier Surinder Singh, Brigadier Operations of the 15 Corps, and they all gave a sharp salute with a 'Jai Hind'. Brig Singh kept moving ahead as others stood waiting for directions. Balhara looked over his glasses at the gang, nodded, waved them forward and went back to his file. 'Give me a minute please,' he said curtly.

Brig Singh, a tall muscular Sikh who was known for spending more time at the gym than anyone else in the Corps HQ, asked the Gorkha team to take their seats on the sofa, while he sat down at the desk, on a chair facing the corps commander. Everyone sat quietly, waiting for Balhara to get free.

Finally, he closed his file, took off his glasses, folded and kept them on the table, smiled at Singh and said, 'Yes, Superman, tell me.'

Singh had earned this nickname due to his ripped, solid build. He always wore shorter sleeves than anyone else to show off his muscular biceps and forearms. But he was also very jovial and friendly, and was one of those rare officers who was loved by everyone up and down the chain of command.

He smiled back and said, 'Sir, the First Four Gorkha Rifles team is here. The operation in Kupwara, where two youngsters killed five foreign terrorists ... you remember? You wanted to meet them, so here they are.'

He pointed towards them, and all three, including Col Deo, stood to attention.

'Oh yes, of course,' Gen Balhara said excitedly, getting up from his chair and walking towards them. Each of them saluted and shook his hand, introducing themselves.

Balhara sat down next to them on a sofa chair and started asking about their unit, area of responsibility, operations, etc. While Col Deo briefed him, Danny nodded along and Deepak just kept praying that no one would speak to him.

'So, these are the two heroes of the operation?' Balhara asked Deo.

'Yes, sir. This is Major Danny Deka, the Delta Company commander, and this is Lt Deepak Lathwal, his company officer, who joined us just a month back,' said Deo, pointing to Danny and Deepak, respectively, who sat on the edge of the sofa.

'Oh good. Another Jat Ram in the room. Welcome Mr Lathwal. So, where are you from?' Balhara asked with a light laugh, leaning back in the sofa chair as he prepared to pull Deepak's leg.

Indian Army personnel have a unique method of addressing each other. Right from their training days, everyone is a 'Jat' or 'Khalsa' or 'Tant' or 'Mallu' and so on. This form of address may not be acceptable or considered politically correct in the civilians' world, but in the armed forces, it is the norm. No one ever feels offended or targeted; rather, mutual insults and pointed racist jokes are what these tough men have bonded over for centuries. It is something impossible for others to understand. It doesn't matter how old you get, the genes that are implanted during training never go away.

Deepak sat bolt upright and said, 'Rohtak, sir. It's in Haryana.'

The moment he uttered the second line, he regretted it.

Balhara leaned forward, put his elbows on his knees, raised his voice and said, 'I know it is in Haryana. You think I am stupid, do you?'

Deepak wished he could die that instant. 'No, sir, I am sorry. I did not mean that. I was just …' He didn't even finish the sentence, going red in the face and moving further and further towards the edge of the sofa, looking set to fall off at any second.

Balhara gave a hearty laugh and waved him to stop. Now, everyone laughed, and Deepak realized it was at his expense. He just blushed some more and smiled weakly.

'So, Danny, tell me about the operation. And later, you can test your company officer on the districts of Haryana,' Balhara said, still smiling.

Danny spent the next fifteen minutes explaining the operation. Once he was done, Balhara asked him, 'What do you think is a good way to track these guys moving across our AOR?'

Danny looked at Deo, who gave a slight nod, and then looked back at Balhara. 'Sir, I command a company in a counterinsurgency role. The area I have to manage is around eight to ten square kilometres of dense forest and mountains. The temperature, terrain, visibility and cliffs make it a very difficult area to monitor constantly. Plus, I have less than a hundred men to manage this vast area. The same troops have to do post protection, admin patrols, cookhouse and other duties, as well as basic area domination daily patrols. How much can I rotate these guys? If I push them too hard, I risk fatigue and demoralization, which will lead to bad combatants and, thus, casualties on our own side. If I try to be a mother and make it too easy for them, the terrorists will have a free run in the area, and, slowly, my troops will also become lethargic and complacent. I am trying my best to maintain a balance, but it is time that our human competence is complimented with technological advancements to give us some edge.'

Balhara looked at Singh and asked, 'Do you want to reply to this?'

Singh nodded and replied, 'Sure, sir. Danny, the Army HQ is working on acquiring some drones at the unit level. The plan is to sync the feed of all units at the formations level so there is no gap in the information. Plus, HQs can share information with ground-level troops when required. You control the drones and use them to cover the area you want to cover, but also carry out a flyby as per formation-level plans. I think it should not take more than eight to ten months to get the drones to the units. The RFPs are already out, and then the usual process of proposal, testing, procurement, etc. follows. The HQs understand your problems and everyone at all levels is working on it. Hope that answers your query.'

Danny looked down at his shoes and stayed silent for a few seconds. Internally, he was contemplating if he should get into this argument or not. But then, Danny being Danny, he looked up and said, 'Sir, what about today and tomorrow? What about every day that troops' lives are at risk—a risk that could be mitigated effectively if we could have the technology that children use to buy from Amazon on a daily basis? Yes, we can buy those tiny quadcopters, given the small budgets units have, but they are hardly effective, given their range and flight time. But we have huge areas to manage. If you can simply increase our budgets for local purchase and allow us to buy better drones, we can be so much more effective on the ground. The long and complicated procurement procedures have been such a bane for the armed forces' operational efficiency. Why are we stuck in this bureaucratic labyrinth? Ground commanders should be given more independence and powers.'

Danny was trying to stay as calm as possible, but his comments were dripping with agitation.

The Corps Commander looked at Singh, whose face was now twisted. He had not expected this retort, and was about to reply when the boss raised his hand for everyone to keep quiet, picked up his phone and spoke into the intercom, 'Please send some tea and cookies for all.'

Then, he turned to look at Danny.

'Danny, you are one of the finest officers we have in our corps zone, or rather, in the entire Army. You have tremendous operational experience and successful operations under your belt. But the Army is much more than just about killing terrorists. Let's say we allow you to buy some drones. Can you guarantee they would not have some Chinese spyware built into them that will share the info with the ISI? Not only will you be sharing your intelligence with them, but also endangering yourself and your boys. The gentlemen sitting in the Army HQ go through all these details and ensure that the equipment that finally comes to the troops is the best, safest and the most economical. It is okay to feel frustrated with the procedures, but trust me, sometimes bureaucracy has its merits. I can assure you that all those sitting in Delhi—and here in Srinagar too—were climbing mountains and jungle-bashing not too long ago. They have not forgotten the problems on the ground, and try their best to make things happen as soon as possible. But no one can change the system. We have to fight within the variables, compete with the cards as they are dealt and win against all odds.'

He waved the tea trolley into the room. The waiter offered everyone tea and the Gorkha team unanimously said 'no'. But Balhara looked at them and hissed, 'Have it.'

All three jumped with a 'yes, sir' and started pouring themselves tea, and even picked up a cookie each. It was delicious Kashmiri kehwa tea and they were glad they had it.

Singh spoke while stirring his tea with a small spoon and looking at Danny. 'I am not contesting your demands and logic. But the Army does not serve one unit or company commander. Any equipment or technology has to be provided to all, to enable everyone, and that too, in a justifiable manner. If we let everyone go for whatever they want and keep funding those demands, we will soon have anarchist mercenaries on our hands. The backbone of the Army is discipline and uniformity. Special concessions can be made in times of emergencies and operational needs. But what you are doing is your duty. Keeping your area free of terrorists and the local population safe and contended is your primary task. There are thousands of company commanders doing the same, day in and day out, as we speak. How can we ignore them?' he asked.

Danny replied immediately, 'But, sir, where is the justice in equality, if you are equating a unit that has killed a hundred terrorists with a unit that has eliminated not even five in two years? Why shouldn't the performers be given the benefits of support? I am sure it will motivate others to do well too.'

Balhara was listening intently to the interaction. He was also an infantry officer, and well known for his troop-friendly stand. He had spent his life making positive changes everywhere he served, and that made him one of the most loved and respected generals in the Army. But he was also known to be a stickler for the rules. According to him, there was no need to cross the line and go renegade to make things happen. He liked slow and steady. In Danny, he saw his opposite—someone eager and desperate, like a skilled player not getting enough to play. Balhara knew the value such soldiers brought to any army; they were rare and needed to be preserved and nurtured, for when war happens, it would be these diehards who win the battles, not the ones who spent time calculating every step and waiting for the situation to be favourable. In his mind, both Singh and Danny were right—they were like the blind men in the adage, holding different parts of the elephant and describing its appearance as a 'rope' or a 'pillar'.

Balhara got up and went to stand beside Singh. Everyone was quiet. He then sat atop his desk and said calmly, 'Deo, Danny and Deepak, you guys are the spearhead of the formation and the Indian Army. You put your lives at risk, lead your brave Gorkhas in battles and deal with daily successes and failures. You know it best and there is no one in this room who argues with that. However, it is imperative that as officers, we understand that we will never have enough.

There is no end to building your fort—every cannon can be bigger and every moat can be wider and deeper. But since the time men picked up sticks to fight each other, people have managed to win battles with whatever they had at their disposal. I do not want this notion to fester that HQs do not take care of you or your needs. Rather, I want you to know that all HQs are very approachable and will do everything possible within their powers to make it happen. But everyone has limits, and everyone is answerable to their bosses. I report to General Abhishek Gera in Udhampur. He reports to the Army chief, who reports to the defence minister. So, as much as we want to just go ahead and buy new surveillance drones or tanks or rifles and have the edge we long for, the process has to be followed each and every time. If we compromise the process, tomorrow there will be such chaos that we will become like the Pakistani military and establishment. They did exactly what is not supposed to be done as uniformed personnel, and look at them today—a country molested by the military, left to rot under fundamentalists' tyranny by weak and corrupt politicians. All because the pillar that holds the nation together, its armed forces, decided to serve themselves before their country. It starts with that first step— why not bend the system to accommodate someone special's demands? Once that door is open, there is no closing it. So, have faith in your system, son. Have some faith.'

Balhara flashed Danny a big smile.

Deepak was absorbing all this and was overwhelmed by the level of the discourse. He could not imagine in his wildest dreams that the corps commander would give them so much space to present their views—he had just been looking forward to a handshake and a pat on the back. But he guessed Gen Balhara was a different breed altogether.

Brig Singh kept his cup on the desk and stood up straight and asked the Gorkhas, 'Gentlemen, if there are no more points, Danny and Deepak can move to the press room. There is this lady who wants to talk to you two about life in operations and all that jazz. She is the daughter of a fallen soldier, so Gen Balhara has agreed to help her with her YouTube channel by allowing these exclusive interviews. Please remember, nothing confidential, nothing operational and nothing personal. Just normal "us good, them bad" stuff. Understood?'

Col Deo, Danny and Deepak stood up and said, 'Yes, sir'. As they began moving towards the door, Balhara queried, 'Deo, have you ever officially initiated this demand for surveillance equipment?'

Deo stepped ahead and replied, 'Yes, sir. Around eight months back, we had sent a statement of case to brigade HQ. But the commander did not find merit in it, and hence I think it was not sent ahead to division and corps.'

'Sorry, who is your brigade commander? I'm forgetting the name,' Balhara asked.

'Brigadier R.K. Srivastav, sir,' Deo responded.

Both Balhara and Singh smiled at each other upon hearing the name, and the commander said, 'Oh, Sandwich Srivastav! No wonder he didn't find merit in your case.' And they both laughed.

The others laughed along too, and Deepak just joined in because he thought he should. He had no idea why the brigade commander had got that nickname and reputation. But if your corps commander cracks a joke and everyone laughs, you join in—no ifs or buts.

The Gorkha trio saluted Balhara and Singh and left the room.

Once they were alone, Balhara said to Singh, 'Solid team, that one.'

Singh nodded. 'Definitely, sir. And that Danny guy, he was the one who did that famous bunker raid around six months back. True daredevil,' he said.

Balhara kept nodding slightly. 'Talk to them periodically. Help them with whatever they need. Make sure they aren't stuck over a few sandbags or satellite photos. Just ensure they are comfortable, administratively and operationally,' he added.

Singh responded with a 'yes, sir', sat down in the chair and pulled out his diary. He had a few other points to discuss with the boss.

8

As Danny and Deepak walked towards the press room, Danny kept a hand on his shoulder and explained to him the sense of humor senior officers have in the army. After he had spoken, Deepak looked at him and said with a naughty smile, 'So sir, when I am not around, it's your backside they flog?' Danny removed the hand from Deepak's shoulder and as he got ready to punch him in the back, Deepak ran ahead laughing. Danny laughed and shouted, 'Run my dear, run now!'

The bond between the two had become rock solid as they had spent a few months together and have gone for missions as a team. A company commander to a younger officer is more than just a senior. He is a friend, brother, father, guide, mentor and every possible version of an elder teacher and protector. But with this strengthening, also comes a whole lot of informality, where the jokes and leg pulling are acceptable and routine.

Danny and Deepak entered the press room and saw a young woman talking animatedly to a man in the middle, next to the chairs placed for when the corps commander briefed the media. Danny couldn't help but notice her long, lean body and beautiful hair that fell loosely over her shoulders. He was about to say something when he noticed that Deepak had already walked ahead with a certain spring in his step. Danny stopped right there, folded his arms in a relaxed posture, and waited to see what the lieutenant was about to do.

Deepak excitedly extended his hand to the reporter. 'Hi, I am Lieutenant Deepak Lathwal from First Four Gorkha Rifles. We were told to meet you here. This … that, is my company commander, Major Danny Deka. We both were in the operation you wanted to talk about. Tell me, how we can help?' he asked, beaming at her.

The journalist jumped to her feet and shook his hand. The man next to her also said 'hello' and ran to the far end of the room to grab his camera and sound equipment.

'So good to meet you, sir. I am Neha Talwar. I am an independent journalist, now freelancing after a few years in the media. I mainly cover defence and Kashmir. I just started my own YouTube channel. Thank you so much for agreeing to talk to me. My father was also in the Army and was General Balhara's coursemate. So, he helps me get some interviews. Uncle has been very kind to me,' she told Deepak, then nodded in the direction of Danny, who calmly nodded back and started walking towards them.

Deepak shook hands with her and signalled everyone to sit down. The men sat on one side and Neha on the other, while the cameraperson behind her fixed his equipment.

'Sir, I am here to get some details, whatever you can share comfortably, about your last operation. General Balhara has this unique policy where instead of him and his staff giving all the briefings, he lets the company commanders talk to the media and give an honest account. I think it's very brave and pioneering of him. Don't you think so?' Neha asked.

Before Danny, the company commander in this scenario, could even open his mouth, Deepak began speaking. He gave a long account of how Gen Balhara had a lot of faith in his unit, and how young officers like him could handle such initiatives responsibly, over and above killing terrorists. Danny noticed that Deepak didn't stop smiling for even a second; his presence was totally lost on the young lieutenant.

Danny tapped Deepak on his shoulder and leaned forward to whisper, 'Calm down, Casanova. Keep some blood in your head as well.' He gave Deepak a stern look. To his shock, Deepak disengaged from the whispering, laughed, slapped Danny's knee and said, 'Of course, sir, I will tell her about what you did too. I was just coming to that.'

Danny wanted to strangle him.

Deepak turned back to Neha. 'Major Danny has to go for an urgent meeting, and he's worried if you'll be okay with just one officer running the briefing,' he said, still smiling at her. She nodded back with a smile on her face too, albeit a confused one.

Deepak looked back at Danny and said, 'Sir, don't worry. If I can kill terrorists, I am sure I can brief the media about it too. You go ahead with your meeting, I will handle this. Please sir, don't be late.'

Danny's teeth were clenched, his eyes narrow. But both he and Deepak knew he would not say anything. So he just got up, brushed his pants, and nodded slowly. 'Fine,' he said. 'I will be waiting with the QRT after my meeting. You take care of this. Just try and wrap up in time.'

Deepak smiled, got up and gave a sharp salute to Danny with a 'yes, sir'. Then, he sat back down and started talking to Neha. Danny waved goodbye to her and resolved to kick Deepak's ass once he met him outside.

* * *

Around two hours later, Deepak came grinning to the QRT, looking triumphant. Danny was sitting in the front passenger seat of the Gypsy, with the door ajar and his feet on the open window, reading a book and having a leisurely smoke. As Deepak greeted him, Danny brought his feet down, called the lieutenant closer, and asked, 'So, how did it go?'

Deepak tapped on his notepad with his index finger and said in a singsong manner, 'Got her phone number.' He smiled like a kid who had just got a new toy.

'You could've taken that from the media cell, idiot. What else? I hope you didn't blab confidential stuff just to get some,' said Danny, alighting from the Gypsy and crushing the cigarette butt.

'No, sir, come on … not at all. Rather, we spent most of the time talking about our personal lives and childhood, etc. I think we both have a lot in common,' he said confidently.

'What both of you have is a lack of common sense. You are ready to blow off your boss to score a hottie, and she is eager to let go of an opportunity to talk to a company commander so she can spend time with a horny idiot who joined hardly a month back. You are made for each other. I just hope your children aren't as ugly as you and as dumb as her,' Danny said, going over to the driver's seat while shaking his head in disbelief.

Deepak got a little irritated, and they had a small argument that lasted for a bit. Then, it was time to leave, and Danny threw away his next cigarette into a roadside drain with a flick of his thumb and index finger. He looked at Deepak and said, 'I don't mind you acting like a hormonal tornado. But the stunt you pulled today also needs to be addressed. The corps commander gave us four sheep and forty chickens as a gift for the company cookhouse. They are loaded in that truck. For our journey back, you will not travel with me in the Gypsy, but sit with them in the rear of the truck. Make sure they are safe and none of them come under terrorist fire. Got it?'

Deepak was about to protest, but stopped himself and said 'yes, sir' instead. He was starting to understand Danny a little better—he was like a great older brother when needed, but also like a strict father when it came to rules and regulations. 'No worries, sir,' he said, walking to the truck. 'I will spend this time writing a letter to my friend Neha.'

Danny shook his head in frustration and shouted, 'Just spare the sheep, you lusty deviant.'

But then, Danny laughed and Deepak frowned. The convoy started its journey back to base with both of them thinking of the women they had in their hearts—one had just met his love, and the other had lost his forever.

9

Just fifteen minutes into the drive, Danny called to Deepak to come sit with him in the Gypsy. Deepak got in smiling and was about to say something when Danny just said with his usual stoicism, 'Shut up and sit.'

And they drove on.

Danny was driving at a leisurely pace, as if using the time to collect his thoughts. They were going back to the unit HQ in Panzgam, while Col Deo had stayed back to have more meetings in the Corps HQ and would return the next day. They had been asked to stay at the unit HQ and meet the CO for lunch before leaving for their post the next day.

Deepak was sitting next to Danny as co-driver, with his AK between his knees, barrel pointed upwards, his hand holding it lightly from the foresight and looking outside the window at the scenery rushing by.

Suddenly, Deepak turned to Danny and said, 'Sir, do you think I should grow a beard and moustache?'

Danny looked at him with visible irritation, then fixed his eyes back on the road and replied, 'No, you are ugly enough anyway.'

Deepak laughed. 'Thank you, sir. But I asked because if we are doing counterterrorist operations, it might help with some cover and camouflage,' he pointed out.

It was common practice among many soldiers deployed in the Kashmir Valley to keep a beard and moustache, or only a beard, to look like the locals. So, Danny let out a sigh and said calmly, 'Sure, go ahead. If you think it's a good idea, why not? But do remember, with a great beard comes great responsibility.'

Deepak laughed again and said, 'So you are a Marvel fan too, sir? Got it. Who is your favourite character?'

Danny made a fist, straightened his arm out over the steering wheel and said, 'Superman. Son of Krypton and saviour of Earth.'

Deepak rolled his eyes and said, 'How cliched, sir. Being a Marvel fan, you're idolizing a DC superhero? Your universes are surely on the path of collision. And who's your favourite Bollywood actor and actress?'

'What is this, a bloody Tinder date?' Danny thundered. He had a tendency to shut down the conversation the moment it began lightening up, but Deepak kept trying his best to loosen him up every chance he got. Exasperated Deepak asked, 'Fine sir, at least tell me which is your favourite drink.'

Danny quietly nodded and said, 'I've always been a big fan of Ballantine's. Somehow I just couldn't connect with rum.'

Deepak, nodding, took out his diary and started writing while mumbling, 'Superman, hates Bollywood, Scotch-drinker, drives slow … hmmm.'

Danny looked at him, and without taking his eyes off him, said, 'You really want to walk to the HQ, right?'

Deepak laughed loudly, kept his diary back in his pocket and said, 'Just taking notes, sir, just taking notes. It is not my intention to irritate you at all. I just want to know my boss a little better. We are a team, sir, a team.' He gave a sly smile.

Danny shook his head in defeat and continued driving.

Again, Deepak surprised him with a sudden question. 'Sir, why is Brigadier Srivastav called "Sandwich Srivastav"?'

Danny smiled a little, looked at the lieutenant and replied, 'My dear D-Cup, as you go through the rigours of military service, you will realize that grenades don't always burst, soldiers aren't always brave and professional excellence is not the only way to get promoted. Brigadier Srivastav and his wife ran a sandwich empire. They were notorious for dropping in at the houses of unsuspecting seniors, loaded with a variety of sandwiches and other eatables. Their proficiency in sandwiches and desperation to entertain is well known— he did not even spare instructors during his courses. Lucky for him, all the seniors through his career appreciated the sandwiches, and he kept getting good grades and ratings. Today, he is commanding a brigade, thanks to white bread and sumptuous fillings. So, the moral of the story is, that there will always be people who will be armed with social, culinary and sycophantic skills that you may not be able to match. The game is to try not to become one of them. Got it?'

'But, sir …'

Danny gave him a sharp look and said, 'Enough. My six-month quota for gossip is over. Focus on the road outside. If someone starts shooting at us, I don't want you distracted with thoughts of sandwiches or that chick you were planning to marry back there in Corps HQ.'

Deepak said, 'Yes, sir,' and started once again to scan the vibrant scenery outside, hoping someone would fire so that he could be a hero again. He was admiring nature when Danny tapped on his leg. He turned his head and looked at Danny and said, 'Yes, sir?'

Danny spoke without taking his eyes off the road. 'I wanted to talk to you about something. Now listen, D-Cup, when you joined the company, you were like a headless chicken and a scared puppy put together. And that's expected. Academy training aside, unit life can be overwhelming in the beginning. But since that encounter, where you got your first kills, you've suddenly transformed from Gangadhar to Shaktiman. Everyone can notice your newfound confidence. And before I say anything else, let me say I'm very happy about it.'

Deepak could see something big was coming but he still managed a weak 'Yes, sir'.

Danny continued, 'But here's a piece of advice from your company commander, senior and brother officer. There is a fine line between confidence and cockiness. Never cross it. Humility is the most important sign of a good person and leader. Doesn't mean I am stopping you from speaking your mind. Also doesn't mean I am giving you the green light to shoot off your mouth brazenly. What I am saying is, we can see you are growing into an able and confident leader. Just don't get lost. Got it?'

Deepak nodded and tightened his lips. He was glad that Danny was there to guide him through his journey and be a mentor. 'I won't let you down, sir. And I'll always remember this.'

Danny nodded and in one of those rare moments, smiled at Deepak and extended his hand. Deepak shook it with all his excitement and said, 'Maybe you can start calling me Deepak, sir.'

Danny laughed loudly and commented, 'Never gonna happen my friend, never.'

They reached Panzgam as the day was about to run out of sunlight.

10

I n any field area deployment, the Officers' Mess is like the trailer of a grand movie. Field units get a much smaller building than they would in a peace deployment area, and they make do with it. The Mess becomes a place where officers get together, dine, chat, drink and are a tad informal with each other.

The tradition of Messes goes back to British times when these buildings were used for bachelors' dining, recreation and accommodation. Nothing much has changed in Messes as far as culture, traditions and etiquettes are concerned. However, there is always some difference in the grandiose manner Messes are set up in peace locations versus the more makeshift ones in field areas.

The 1/4 Gorkha Rifles, with its nearly 175 years of history, had so much to display that no unit Mess building in any cantonment could accommodate all its trophies, medals, paintings, battle honour shields, etc. Originally commissioned as the 'Prince of Wales's Own Gorkha Rifles', the first battalion of the Fourth Gorkha Rifles had proven its worth across continents—in both World Wars, all of India's wars, and in counterterrorism operations in the Northeast and Kashmir. The unit, with its rich traditions, was considered one of the most disciplined and ethical in the entire Indian Army. All officers and men who had ever served in it always felt fortunate to be part of its history.

With the number of terrorists killed in this tenure, the unit was sure to get another feather in the cap—the Chief of Army Staff's citation.

The field Mess had a large seating room, a dining room, a small room turned into a library, a kitchen and a couple of others being used as guest rooms. It had only a limited number of trophies on display—the most important and historic ones. Every young officer joining the unit is supposed to learn all about the unit and regiment's history, and also know the history behind every trophy, flag and medal. Deepak was already wondering how he would learn all this. He was happy to hunt terrorists in jungles and did not mind the hardships, but learning about battles, dates and the important soldiers was stressing him out. He had seen the Mess the day he joined, and was told in no uncertain terms that the sooner he learnt all this, the better it would be for him. When he asked Danny if he knew everything about regimental history, he replied curtly, 'More than you.'

Deepak realized even Danny wasn't too good at this, so maybe he could hide behind him and not have to go through this ordeal.

Lt Col Ankush Sharma saw Danny and Deepak talking and shouted out from the middle of the main room, 'Hey Danny, bring your D-Cup here.'

Danny laughed and pushed Deepak toward the group of officers having beers in the anteroom. 'Hey D-Cup, hope you aren't too "pressed" for time,' said Sharma, and everyone in attendance laughed.

Deepak just kept looking down and nodding. Then, he raised his head and said with a smile, 'No, sir. I am in good shape. Firm and bouncy.'

Everyone laughed again, and Sharma patted Deepak on his back. 'That's the spirit, my boy! Don't let anyone squeeze you whenever they want,' he said.

Then, he turned to Danny and asked, 'So, Danny, how did Deepak become D-Cup?'

Danny looked at Deepak and said, 'Sir, actually it was the radio guy's innocent mistake. One day during an operation, he pronounced it "Dee-cup saab", and it caught on.'

Everyone laughed and cracked some more jokes about Deepak. By now, he was learning to take them in his stride. As the youngest member of the team, he knew these men would always take care of him, but wouldn't hesitate to tear him apart when it came to making fun of him. Also, the fact that he had carried out a successful operation and had a few kills under his belt not only gave him a lot of confidence, but also made others look at him as a dependable and solid soldier.

At that moment, Col Deo entered, and everyone greeted him and fell silent. He sat down and asked everyone to take their seats and started talking about regular unit affairs. Soon, everyone was having a glass of beer and freshly steamed momos, talking about a variety of topics. Deepak observed that Danny never talked much in such gatherings. Well, he never talked much anyway. But once in a while, he would just mutter something to prove he was present.

The CO finally asked if everyone was ready to have lunch and excused himself to go to the washroom.

And that is when it happened.

A loud bang shook the entire building and even caused a couple of paintings to fall down. The windows rattled wildly, and the glasses fell on the tables they had been kept on. Everyone assembled jumped onto the floor with their arms covering their heads. Dust started to cascade slowly from all corners of the Mess.

Deepak had never heard something so loud. He was also lying down, covering his head and trying to see what the others were doing so that he could follow. Col Deo came running, still zipping up his pants, and shouted, 'Adjutant, announce stand-to for the entire unit. Everyone at their positions with weapons. Get QRTs assembled in the MT area. All company commanders, get your teams ready. And where is Danny?'

Everyone realized Danny was missing, and Col Deo shouted his name again. Deepak suddenly felt responsible; he got up and said, 'Sir, I'll look for him.'

'No! You gather your boys and assemble in the MT area. This sounded like an IED blast very close to the unit area. Let's stay coordinated, Danny will turn up,' CO shouted his directions quickly.

By now, everyone was up and running outside to gather their weapons, shouting directions to their teams while scrambling between the vehicles waiting to take them back to their companies after lunch. It was chaos. But Deepak was still wondering where Danny was.

He reached his team, and asked, 'Where is Danny sir?'

The guy standing in the jeep with the mounted LMG said he'd run towards the main gate with two boys, and asked the rest to wait there. This meant that when everyone had jumped to take cover and were wondering what was happening, Danny had already scooted with two of his boys to investigate. Deepak was impressed but also angry, wondering why he hadn't taken him. Somehow that was his primary concern at that point.

He jumped into the QRT vehicle and asked his team and driver to move towards the gate. The senior company JCO Subedar Vikas Rana said, 'Sir, but all teams have been asked to move to the MT area. That is where CO saab will be.'

'We will go to the gate. That is where our Danny saab will be,' he said authoritatively. Within seconds, the team had jumped into the vehicles they had bought along as their company convoy and sped towards the gate.

11

Deepak's team took around two minutes to reach the main gate of the unit area. They found Danny in one of the pill boxes, talking to the guard. The jeeps screeched to a halt and the men jumped out of the vehicles and ran towards the gate. Within seconds, everyone had taken cover behind the pillars and the gate, pointing their AKs towards the main road.

Danny spotted Deepak and shouted, 'What are you doing here?'

Deepak didn't know how to answer. What kind of question was that? Where else was he supposed to go if not to his company commander? He barely managed a 'sir'.

Danny's face calmed. He patted Deepak on the cheek and said, 'Good boy. Now listen, there was a big IED blast hardly two hundred metres from the gate. It was a vehicle IED, most probably meant for our gate. We were lucky the guys inside panicked or something went wrong and it blew up sooner. But that doesn't mean we are out of the woods. The way terrorists operate is that they send one vehicle to blast the gate and then others to storm inside the camp. Thankfully, the gate is still intact, and the guards are unharmed. But who knows what will happen next. You man the gate here and I'll organize the defences. Don't move, got it?'

Danny ran towards the team and quickly gave some directions, and the troops started to take positions. He took around five minutes to get his team and the guards at the gate into a solid defensive position. By this time, the guard commander had updated the CO on the phone about the situation. Help must be on its way, Deepak thought.

He was right. Within minutes, he saw loads of troops and vehicles coming towards the gate. Soon, all the men had taken position and were ready to face anything that tried to come through.

Five intense minutes passed, with everyone's cheeks glued to their rifles and eyes peering down the iron sights of their rifles. Nothing happened. But the failed plan was a dead giveaway that something or someone out there had bigger and more menacing plans. This could easily go on till the next morning, and everyone knew it too well.

A HQ or base generally does not have a large fighting force—most combatants are deployed as part of the rifle companies engaged in counterterrorism operations. Apart from people going on leave or returning, the majority of manpower at the base is clerical, transportation and administration-related. All of these are soldiers, but may or may not be as trained in combat as GD soldiers. These tradesmen are given basic training but spend their lives doing their primary jobs.

The base also has the commanding officer's QRT and Ghatak platoon, if they are not out for any operation. Guard duties are divided among all of them, and defending the fort often falls on the shoulders of these men. Although a unit's base has anywhere between seventy to a hundred combatants at any given time, they are not as organized as they are in their respective companies on the posts. So while the number might look large, the lack of coordinated tactical deployment is a major drawback while carrying out even defensive operations such as this.

Terrorists knew this as well, but what they didn't know was that because Col Deo had organized a debriefing and all company commanders had come down to the base to attend it, the cream of the unit was present there that day. Each company commander always had a crack team of fifteen to twenty men with him whenever moving outside his company post—his convoy protection plus personal QRT guys. Needless to say, they usually are the sharpest and quickest in their respective companies. Today, apart from the base troops, there were close to eighty of these soldiers and their commanders with extensive experience in hunting terrorists.

Thus, the tables were about to be turned. The terrorists who came to surprise the base were in for a very nasty surprise themselves. Everyone held their positions for nearly an hour. However, nothing else seemed to be moving. The police team had already reached the IED blast site and was trying to scrape the remains of the vehicle and bodies off the road.

Col Deo knew it was a futile bureaucratic procedure and no intelligence could be gathered from that. He was more worried about what was lurking in the village just across the road.

He called all the company commanders back to his office, leaving the company officers in charge of the stand-to. There, he spread out a map on his table, pointed at the village just opposite the base HQ and said, 'We need to kill this threat as soon as possible. I think they are waiting for the dark now. Sharma, you lay the outer cordon for the village. Ashwani, your team will cover all exit routes. Vishal and Danny, you will start the search inside the village from one axis each. Take your teams and get going ASAP. Adjutant, you'll review the base defence once again and manage it. Surpal, if you don't mind, can you man the communications and stay in touch with brigade HQ? They will start asking for updates every minute very soon, and I don't want them bothering me.'

Lt Col Surpal Singh was the second-in-command of the unit, and had just joined a couple of months back after a tenure at Army HQ. A very bright up-and-comer, he knew exactly how to handle the higher HQs.

Everyone discussed the details quickly and left the room. All these guys had done hundreds of operations, and getting into action just came naturally to them.

Teams were called and briefings were given. Soon, everyone had mounted the vehicles. Col Deo had decided they would take the road that bypassed the village and reached the other end. This would allow the vehicles to leave from a gate far away from the one in view of the village, not only to maintain the element of surprise, but also to not lead his own guys into a direct ambush if the terrorists were watching the main gate after the IED blast.

It was 4.30 p.m., and soon, it would start to get dark in the town of Panzgam, deep in the valley of Kashmir. A blown-up car lay billowing smoke from burning leather close to the gate of the base, with two charred bodies inside it. Police would be handling the removal and postmortem, as per the protocol.

12

Maj Vishal Parmar was the commander of the Charlie Company. A native of Gurugram, he was one of the finest soldiers in the unit, and had received the Sena Medal during his tenure in the Rashtriya Rifles (RR).

He was the coolest cat Col Deo had at his disposal—complicated situations did not stress Vishal but brought out the best in him. Deo deliberately teamed him up with Danny to do the house-to-house search, as he could not think of a better team of field operatives and commanders to lead this complicated race against time. Deo wanted to eliminate those hiding in the village as soon as possible. They could escape into the deep jungles behind the village at any time, and he would forever lose the chance to discover their plan. For him, it was a really big deal that the terrorists could even dare to plan and launch an attack against his unit.

Accompanying Vishal was his company officer, Captain Amol Lawate. A lanky young lad who was infamous for having more girlfriends than all the other officers combined, Amol was a true daredevil who often had to be restrained from running guns blazing into a hailstorm of bullets. He was exceptional in the field, and had also received instructor gradings in his young officer course. The CO had high hopes for him as he had all the makings of a great officer. He intentionally kept him under Vishal to teach him more about patience and control.

Amol was Deepak's senior subaltern in the unit. There was no one between them, so Amol was responsible for his grooming, teaching him about the unit's traditions and culture, and ensuring his well-being. The unit had this beautiful tradition that created unbreakable brotherly bonds between two officers, that transcended time and distance. Deepak, for example, would often call Amol whenever he wanted to clarify any doubt or needed some help. Even though Danny was his company commander, the formality of that relationship prevented him from asking naïve questions.

Deepak leaned towards Amol as they travelled in an MPV and whispered, 'Sir, have you ever done house searches?'

'Yes,' replied Amol. 'It is one of the most complicated and risky operations. But don't worry, just follow what Major Danny says. He is the best there is. Just follow him and learn.'

He patted Deepak's back and smiled.

Their commanders, Danny and Vishal, were having a serious discussion a bit further towards the front of the MPV. These vehicles were like compact trucks, with seating in the rear on two sides along the length and thus, all the troops sit facing each other, covered in bulletproof jackets and helmets, weapons between their legs, grenades and extra ammo in pouches and khukris hanging at the hip. They looked like a deadly bunch indeed.

The radio guy kept mumbling something into his mouthpiece once in a while, apparently checking range and connectivity with other parties and the base. The radio communication was always in Nepali—that too, hardcore slang from the eastern part of that country which only boys from that particular area could speak and understand; it was a slang that not even regular Nepali-speaking men and officers could understand. This was just an added layer of security in communication, lest someone was eavesdropping.

The vehicles were moving at breakneck speed. There was no time to lose. They had already skirted past the village and would be reaching their designated location soon. Danny and Vishal asked their teams to check their equipment and be ready to dismount. Within the next five minutes, the MPV screeched to a halt and everyone got down and took cover. The search teams were going to hold and wait for the cordon parties to signal that they were in position. Only when the trap was set would the hunters move.

It was nearly dark, and the radio operator, Naik Nar Bahadur, informed Danny, 'Sir, Alpha and Bravo in position.'

Danny nodded, looked at Vishal and asked, 'You ready, Guruji?'

Vishal smiled, cocked his rifle and responded, 'Always, sir, always.'

They signalled to their teams to move. They had no idea if they were laying a trap or walking into one, but these Gorkha daredevils had made a habit of thinking about both scenarios in the same way—just walk ahead and face whatever comes, and simply slash your way out with Khukris shining.

13

anny sat in a chair, sipping hot tea, watching the Sarpanch of the village give directions to residents about the search operation. The Gorkha team was behind providing cover all around him, and Deepak was standing behind, watching the proceedings intently.

In a planned search operation, the military commander asks the sarpanch to inform the residents to come out and gather at one place—usually the local community hall or school—and stay there till the search is over. This minimizes the risk of civilian casualties during the search, making it clear to the search party that anyone inside a house is not a resident. One team checks the villagers' IDs and ensures that no unwanted guest is hiding among them.

It took around an hour for all the villagers to vacate their houses and reach the local school. Vishal's JCO and his team started checking IDs, which led to a lot of angry words being thrown around by the villagers in Kashmiri. Even those who didn't know a word of the language could understand what they meant—it is impossible to ask people to move out of their cosy homes on a cold night, or even in summer, and not expect them to feel resentment towards the Army. But someone has to do the job, and on this day, it was the responsibility of these few men.

Vishal and Amol started the search from the south, and Danny and Deepak began searching the houses from the north. The same drill, house after house—it was mundane and boring, and there was no sign of any untoward elements.

Danny saw Deepak slouching near the door of one of the houses and talking to his men, who had just finished searching it. He called Deepak over and put his arm around his shoulder, leading him away from the troops. A few feet ahead, he asked Deepak, 'Do you know the number one reason for Army deaths in Kashmir?'

'Terrorist activities,' said Deepak.

'No, complacency. Every time you are lazy, unaware or careless, you become a target. That is what they want. There is no break from being sharp and cautious, Deepak, because if you are not, either you or your men will buy it,' said Danny. 'Don't think they are not watching you. Don't think they do not notice how each officer or leader acts. Their informers are everywhere. They have their eyes and ears on us, even as we stand here talking to each other. You cannot stop them from attacking you, but you can definitely make sure they don't succeed. Especially in operations, I want your senses at 110 per cent.'

'Sorry sir, I will take care,' said Deepak, walking back to his team briskly. He gave them some orders and they moved on to the next house.

Houses in North-Kashmiri villages are typically made of a mix of wood, cement and bricks. In general, you open the front door and enter a large living room, which serves as the family's common room and where guests are entertained. There is always an upstairs section accessible with wooden steps, and on top of that is the sloping roof, a hallmark of buildings in the hills.

These are not easy houses to search, especially because they are not brightly lit. Upon entering, it takes a few seconds for the eyes to adjust to the dim light, so if there is someone inside waiting, he has all the time to hit the entering party very comfortably from behind cover. Terrorists who know they are surrounded and see search parties coming in often wait for this moment to hit the armed forces as hard as they can before the gun battle starts. Hence, entering the house and going up the stairs is by far the riskiest manoeuvre in the entire universe of counterterrorist operations.

Danny, of course, knew this. He had his own houses to search and stay attentive to, but kept one eye on Deepak, who he knew was a little distracted. It was Deepak's first search operation and Danny had never got the time to teach him properly about tactics and movement. They had just landed right in the middle of this mayhem. And Danny wished they had enough time today so he could take Deepak step by step through the procedures and tactics.

He was still thinking about this when he entered the next house. Nar Bahadur tapped him on the shoulder and passed the handset to him with the words 'D-Cup saab'.

Danny took the handset, pressed the lever and said, 'Yeah? Over.'

'D-Cup for Delta-1. Movement detected. Green house next to the bus stop. Over.'

When the whole unit was in operation, Danny could not use the 'Tiger' callsign, because it was reserved for the CO. He, thus, became 'Delta-1'. But, sadly, for Deepak, he was stuck with D-Cup and everyone enjoyed calling him that.

'Good. Stay in cover. Reaching in five. Out.'

Danny rushed outside and signalled to his team to follow him. Within minutes, he was beside Deepak, who told him his scout Tej Bahadur, saw movement in the upstairs window of the house with the green roof.

'What did you see?' Danny asked, Rifleman Tej Bahadur.

'Someone just moved away from the window, sir. He was wearing a grey pheran. I couldn't see his face or if he had a gun or not.'

Danny nodded and continued, 'Deepak, you take four boys and get to the windows in the house right behind the green-roofed one. Cover it fully from one side. One team of two boys will stay here at the bus stop. One team of four will go across the road behind those trees. I will send six of my boys on the other side of the house, covering from that side. I will go in with the remaining three and radio. I will also ask Vishal to send additional guys and cover the gaps. Once everyone is in place, we search the house. Got it?'

Deploying troops came naturally to Danny. In his mind, he could draw the whole place like a diagram and then start filling gaps with men and guns. He never hesitated to call for reinforcements. 'It's a resource, always use it. What immature leader does not use all his resources to ensure victory?' he would often tell Deepak when they discussed operations.

'Yes, sir, understood. But can I come with you for the house entry? I want to see how it's done,' Deepak asked meekly.

Danny didn't want to dissuade him, but it was never a good idea for two officers of the same company to enter a dangerous situation together, because the aforementioned first volley from the terrorists could take them both out. But if he didn't take Deepak along, how else would he teach him? If it was to be baptism by fire, so be it. Plus, he felt a little more confident after Deepak's performance in the last operation. The lad can hold his ground, he thought.

'Fine, you come with me. But no Rambo shit. Just follow what you're told and move from cover to cover,' he told Deepak.

Then, he looked at his CHM Vishnu Thapa. 'Vishnu, you take four guys and take up position in the house instead of Deepak saab,' he instructed.

A veteran of tons of operations, Vishnu had also done a stint as an instructor at the CIJW School. He was as good as they came, and was one of Danny's most trusted NCOs.

Young Vishnu had been a rifleman for just month when he received the Shaurya Chakra; he'd jumped from a twenty-foot-high rock face onto two fleeing terrorists, and though his AK had fallen away upon landing, he'd slayed them both with his khukri. He was a legend in the unit, the life of the party with his Nepali dance, and the nemesis of terrorists in Kupwara.

'Yes, sir!' Vishnu replied smartly to his leader's order.

Deepak was smiling like a child at the chance to go with Danny into the house. He also said, 'Yes, sir!'

Danny rolled his eyes and moved away to call Vishal on the radio. He explained the situation. Vishal immediately asked Amol to join Danny's team with ten boys. Next, Danny informed the CO and all the companies who were in the cordon to stay alert. Now, he was just waiting for Amol to show up with his team, and for the other parties to get into place.

It was time for the next formality before entering the house. Danny called the team stationed with the villagers in the school, and asked them to bring the owner of the green-roofed house to him.

Within a few minutes, Amol had arrived, and his team had taken position on two sides, covering both flanks of the house. Two guys accompanied the house owner from the school to Danny's location.

'Not this clown,' Danny muttered to Deepak. Then he got up, went to the house owner, shook hands and hugged him, and brought him back to where Deepak and his team were hiding.

'Mushtaq ji, this is Lieutenant Deepak. He has just joined the unit and is now in my company. Deepak, this is Mushtaq Lone, an apple farmer and an old friend of the unit and the Army.'

Deepak said hello and Mushtaq responded with a big namaste and a bigger bow—something that would put even

Japanese greetings to shame. He then walked to Deepak, hugged him warmly and said, 'Welcome to Kashmir, sir. We are very lucky to have the Gorkha Rifles protecting us. I must tell you…'

'Yeah, yeah, Mushtaq ji,' said Danny, cutting him off. 'Let's catch up later. Just tell me if there is anyone in the house. My boys saw some movement.' He knew very well that once he started speaking, there was no stopping him.

'Oh, no, no, no. Impossible, sir ji,' Mushtaq said, now with elaborate, almost Italian hand gestures. 'There is absolutely no one in the house. I asked both my wives and all four children to move to the school the moment we heard the announcement. You know I am always very sincere with Army drills. I am always…'

'Okay,' said Danny, cutting him off again. 'But we will enter the house and check it now. You wait here with these boys you came with.'

Mushtaq's face fell immediately. He knew what would happen to his house in case there was someone inside. He said, pleadingly, almost on the verge of tears, 'Sir, please take care of my house.'

Danny put his hand on the villager's shoulder. 'Mushtaq ji, I could take you in front of me as cover. I could start a firefight from outside and fire a few rockets into your house and burn it down, just because there are terrorists inside. I could even ransack your house when I am inside, just to search for anything. But we are the Gorkhas. Have you ever heard of us taking civilians as cover? Have you ever heard of us destroying a house just on suspicion? No. If there is danger, we will face it and eliminate it. Rest assured that nothing will happen to your house as long as it is within my control,' he said calmly.

'Thank you, sir. Thank you very much. I will wait here. And once your operation is over, please have tea and some snacks at my home,' Mushtaq replied gently.

'Sure, sure,' Danny replied, smiling and pressing Mushtaq's shoulder reassuringly once again. He asked about the layout of the house, which seemed pretty standard, though he did make a note when Mushtaq said he had a huge wooden almirah meant for storage in the attic, which was empty right now. Danny asked the two boys who had accompanied Mushtaq from the school to take position behind the bus stop and keep him with them.

He turned to Deepak. 'It's time to move. Any questions?'

'Yes, sir. Is he not a good guy? You were cursing when he came up. Should we believe him that there is no one in the house?'

'Okay, D-Cup, listen. First, I don't like him because he talks a lot. And I mean a *lot*—like a politician fighting an election. Otherwise, he has been a good chap. Second, never trust anyone. You will go mad trying to find the truth, and you will realize it does not matter at all. People can act as your friends for decades here and still support terror activities and never get caught. But he could also be genuine and ignorant about someone being inside his house. Maybe the team positioned outside the village forced these guys here, and they entered the house after the villagers moved to the school. We will talk to Mushtaq later and see if he knows something. But

I don't see much coming from it. Most probably, even he doesn't know who is in his house or how. Maybe the terrorists lured, threatened or promised him something. There is no point in analyzing that. What matters is, is there someone inside or not? If yes, how do we go in and come out alive, after having killed them all? Makes sense?'

Danny's small tutorial was taken in very sincerely by Deepak, who just nodded and replied, 'Yes, sir.'

'Let's move. I'll take the lead and you follow after the radio, then the rest of the team. Jai Mahakali!' Danny said sharply.

Then, he moved the safety catch on his rifle to 'fire' and started walking towards the house. Everyone followed, crouched, leaving a little gap from the guy ahead.

It was a night Deepak would come to remember as the one when he started worshipping Danny.

14

Danny was bleeding profusely from one leg, having fallen behind a big wooden sofa in the living room. His radio operator, Nar Bahadur Thapa, was lying face down in a pool of blood; wisps of smoke rising from bullet holes in the radio set. Deepak had been able to enter the room but had to jump behind a big wooden chair the moment he heard the first burst of AK fire. The others behind him immediately took cover outside the door and saved themselves from the hail of bullets aimed at the door.

The room was full of smoke. There was shouting and violent, noisy gunfire from the terrorists. Deepak's heart was in his mouth, and he was just hunched behind the chair, clutching his AK and having no idea where the gunfire was coming from. He wanted to take a peek, but he knew it could be his last. His mind was numb and his legs were shaking. He kept telling himself, 'Focus. Focus. Focus.'

Danny was hit just below the knee. Thankfully the bullet had gone through his calf and did not shatter his bone. But it did tear off a huge lump of flesh. Danny was in excruciating pain and losing blood very fast. He knew the fire had come from the stairs, which meant the enemy was in the attic. But even getting up now and leaving the cover meant sureshot target practice for the bad guys. He looked at his radio operator, who was either dead or maybe about to die, and felt all his anger and frustration rise. He gathered his thoughts and decided to take charge. There will be time to feel the pain, he thought to himself. With the constant firing from the terrorists in the attic and the counter-firing at the door by his guys, he knew that his team had not been able to enter the house. He was worried about Deepak but did not want to shout and ask anything that could give their positions away.

'I have to take charge now,' he decided firmly and took off his belt to tie a tourniquet around his thigh to help with the bleeding. He took out a first-aid kit from his pouch, wrapped the battlefield dressing around his wound, and almost fainted from the pain. He then shoved a few painkiller tablets into his mouth. Though not part of an authorized medical kit, he always kept some with him. And rightly so!

The moment Danny had entered the house, he had known something was off. His eyes had immediately gone to the stairs, where he saw a guy crouched with an AK. Danny had rushed to take cover behind the large sofa in the room and shouted 'cover' to those following. But before he could get the word out, he heard the crack of the AK and felt something rip his leg. He fell forward, and in a second, the worst pain imaginable took over his senses. He looked at his leg and saw it covered in blood. Just behind him, he saw his radio operator lying face down, his radio set shot to smithereens.

Now, after having given himself first aid, Danny immediately started thinking about the messy situation he was in. The shooter was on the stairs leading to the attic. 'He isn't a very well-trained shooter or he would have been able to get me in the head or chest,' he concluded. 'Maybe he was firing at a moving target for the first time, so he tried to adjust for his high position and fired really low, hitting my leg. His weak grip made his AK shake and move, and his volley of bullets turned in an upward arc, hitting my radio guy in the chest or face just behind me. So, I have a scared novice in front of me. And if he is their lead gunman and there are others behind him, they can't be better than him. Time to test my theory.'

He knew that trapped terrorists would fight to their death, because there was no escape, and they would want to take out as many security personnel as they could. Sometimes, they would even grab a grenade with its pin out, so that when their bodies were being moved after death, the grenade would blow up and kill the troops moving the bodies. It was a typical 'us-versus-them' situation Danny found himself in. Neither side had the option to retreat, but only one would get out of this house alive, that was sure.

Danny thought of lobbing a grenade onto the stairs, but that had a high chance of not reaching the target, or bouncing off and falling on the living room floor, where it could end up injuring himself or Deepak. God only knew where Deepak was hiding. The only way to stop that terrorist from firing like a maniac was to make him retreat to the attic, so the team could take their positions.

Danny crawled forward a little, and tried to peep from the side of the sofa. There was a huge chair blocking the view. He crawled back and peeped from the other side of the sofa, where he could see the stairs partially. The centre table was blocking the view this time, and he would have to get up a bit if he wanted to see more. He decided to take the risk, pulled his leg towards him with both hands and winced as he got into a crouch.

He waited to hear how the terrorist was firing at the door—three or four-round bursts every few seconds. Clearly, his aim was to not let more guys enter. None of the bullets were hitting the sofa, so the terrorist must have assumed that he had killed them both with his first burst. That was good news to Danny—he did not have the terrorist's attention, and he would take full advantage of it.

Danny waited for the next burst from the guy on the stairs, got his AK to his shoulder, placed his cheek on its butt and waited out the pause. The moment he heard the next burst, he got up in a flash, rifle in position, saw the guy on the stairs and pressed the trigger. He had learnt from experience that the best time to fire at an enemy was when he was firing, because his complete attention would be on aiming at his target and he would be blind to anyone else popping up on the scene. In this case, Danny.

The terrorist got hit on both his legs and shouted loudly as he tumbled down the stairs like a rag doll. As he reached the bottom, his AK fell far away. He was howling in pain, clutching his legs close to his chest. Danny could see his head bobbing up and down in pain. He took steady aim and slammed two in his head. It came to rest permanently.

Danny jumped and took cover behind the big chair next to the sofa; he now had a better view of the room, with an eye on the stairs. He shouted loudly to his team, 'Get inside and take cover. Deepak, where are you?'

* * *

Deepak was still crouching behind a heavy teak chair in the far end of the room, and had no idea what was going on. Then he heard the guy on the stairs shouting and tumbling, and seconds later, two shots. He peeped from one side of the chair and saw the young terrorist's face—eyes still, blood spurting out of his mouth and nose, hair matted across the forehead, body in a grotesque pose. Deepak did not know what to feel except relief that he was dead.

Then, he heard Danny shouting for him. He raised his AK above the chair and shouted back, 'Sir, here!'

The team finally rushed inside and took cover behind chairs, the sofa and other pieces of furniture. A lot of men were now inside, but they didn't know how many terrorists were in the attic. Danny asked Deepak to come over and gave directions to the others to aim at the stairs and shoot the moment they see a foot coming down.

He then went to his radio operator and rolled his body over. Deepak had also joined him by this time. They crouched next to their departed colleague and then looked at each other. Danny sent a guy outside to use another radio set belonging to Amol's team to inform the HQ that they had lost one of their own, and that one terrorist was dead. 'The search is still on, and I will update on progress later,' he said. The guy left immediately to pass on the message.

'He was exceptionally brave today. He killed the terrorist and saved our lives, even if it meant sacrificing his own,' Danny said solemnly.

Deepak, looking at the departed radio operator, said in surprise, 'But, sir, I saw him fall down ahead of me the moment we entered.'

'He was exceptionally brave today. He killed the terrorist and saved our lives, even if it meant sacrificing his own,' Danny repeated firmly.

'Yes, sir. Understood,' Deepak paused for a second, and then nodded knowingly.

Danny nodded back and tried to get up. It was then that Deepak saw the blood and the bandage on his leg. He was shocked and almost overcome with a sense of guilt that his company commander had been hit and he had done nothing about it. 'Sir, what happened? Are you okay? Let's go outside and call the nursing assistant,' he blurted out with a serious sense of urgency.

Danny looked at him, pointed to the radio operator's body and said, 'Not till we finish what started this. Now stop being a mommy and let's clear the attic.'

Danny limped across the room to reach near the stairs. He did not want to step on them and become an easy target for the terrorists, should there be any more. So, he just lobbed a grenade upstairs and asked two of his guys to do the same. Both of them threw a couple of grenades upstairs and the blasts could be heard across the village.

There was no noise, no firing, no shouting from the attic. Danny inched up the stairs, looking directly ahead through the sight of his AK, ready to fire at anyone who came into view. Deepak followed him closely, with the team behind. When they reached upstairs and started scanning, they found a large haversack with a small bag next to it, which seemed like it belonged to the terrorist lying dead downstairs.

'Check, maybe it has the address of seventy-two virgins,' Danny said with a smile. It was now clear that there was only one terrorist hiding in the house, and he had been eliminated. Vishnu and the other teams also reported that they did not notice any movement or anyone jumping from the windows. The rest of the house had been searched and nothing was found.

Danny asked one of his soldiers to call a radio operator inside, so he could report to the CO. He sat down on a sack of grains and rested his back against the wall. Suddenly, he started to feel very tired. The pain had begun rising again as the adrenalin subsided, and other human feelings came flooding back too. He signalled for Deepak to come to him and said, 'I think I have lost a lot of blood. I might faint after some time. Talk to the CO, update him and get me a doctor ASAP. And take control of the situation. Don't fuck it up.'

Danny realized it was time to rest his eyes. He didn't know it would be a long time before he opened them again.

15

What qualities do you need to be a good leader? Deepak found himself pondering when he reached the base after the operation in the village. Danny had been shifted to the Base Hospital in Srinagar and was getting treated for the gunshot wound by some of the best doctors not only in the Army but also in the country. He was out of danger, but it would be a few weeks before he could be back in action, and even then, it might take a couple of months for his wounds to heal properly and for him to be in fighting shape.

A lot is taught in academies about leadership—right from day one at the NDA, everyone talks about being a good leader. But who decides who is a good leader?

A leader who's very popular among his followers could be morally corrupt, and overall evil. A very unpopular leader might just be result-focused, someone who pushes everyone hard and thus ends up being not liked. A leader trying to balance work and play might not even be remembered after some time because he never strongly advocated for any particular position.

So where does the answer lie?

Having spent some time with Danny in the field and operations, Deepak could not think of one flaw in him—he led by example, he was one of the best in his profession, he always put his team before himself, and he listened to everyone's problems and stepped up to solve them. He was intelligent, perceptive and highly empathetic. Deepak thought of all the qualities taught at the academy and realized that Danny not only possessed them all, but also added a few of his own to the list.

After what happened in the village, Danny had left a deep impression on Deepak's psyche—especially the part where he made a hero out of Nar Bahadur, his radio operator, without worrying about personal glory. Danny set the bar so high that Deepak was sure he would never be able to match it. Naik Nar Bahadur would now get a gallantry award, much better compensation for his family and maybe even a better pension.

Surprisingly, when Deepak told this story to Col Deo while updating him in his office, the CO only asked one thing, 'Did you see the radio operator kill the terrorist, or did Danny tell you?'

'Sir, Major Danny told me. I was hiding behind the chair when the firing was on,' Deepak clarified.

'Figures,' said Deo with a smile, patting Deepak on his shoulder before moving to sit down in his chair. 'There are men and then there is Danny. There are leaders and then there is Danny. There are idiots and then there is Danny. Just remember to learn the right things from him. There is no match for him when it comes to being a soldier, but he has a little self-destructive streak when it comes to his career. Learn from him, but also teach him to calm down at times. You two are more than brothers now, and there will be times when you will have to play a much bigger role than just being a junior officer. Anyway, well done. The whole unit is proud of you.'

'You will accompany the body of Naik Nar Bahadur to his house for the last rites. It is our duty as officers to meet the family and hand over the mortal remains and national flag, pay our respects and ensure that proper military honour is given. The adjutant will brief you in detail. Take care.'

Deepak nodded, but said, 'Sir, can I ask you something? We can see that there is a lot of activity happening in the area. Shouldn't I go back to the company and focus on operations?'

Col Deo took a couple of deep breaths and leaned back in his chair. Neither said anything for a few seconds. Deepak could sense he had made a big mistake and, 'Sir, if Major Sukhinder could go instead—because he is in the medical category right now for his ankle fracture, and not operating—I could be of…'

The CO cut him off. 'I am happy that you are so keen on operations, Deepak. That's commendable. But always remember that terrorists will come and go and operations will keep happening, but the bond we share with our men is to be built with a lot of effort, and then nurtured all through your life. Your men go hunting with you, they follow your command without thinking twice, and like in this case, a man lost his life working with you. We owe it to these men as their leaders to meet and console their families, and to ensure the best benefits are given to them ASAP. This casualty happened in your operation. A soldier from your company died fighting alongside you. Don't you think it's your duty as a soldier, leader and a good human being to visit the family and tell them about how brave their son was? That you were there to hold his hand when he breathed his last?'

Deepak was not expecting the conversation to get so intense—he had gone in assuming it would be a clear yes or no. He thought he was making the right call by trying to focus on operations. But he gathered his wits and replied, 'You are right, sir. I did not think of it. I'm sorry. I will accompany Nar Bahadur's mortal remains to his village in Dehradun.'

'Yes, you should,' replied the CO. 'I told you all this to make you understand that we are not robots just meant to fire at bad guys and keep roaming around in the jungles to find them. As an officer of one of the oldest and finest units of the Indian Army, you are much more than just a terrorist-hunting tool. Do you understand what I'm trying to say?'

Deepak nodded vigorously and let out a very military 'yes, sir!' and sat straight in his chair.

Col Deo continued, 'Very soon, you will find yourself in a position where your troops and junior officers will look to you for guidance and decisions. You will have to make choices that aren't easy. Every step you take, every small or big decision you make, you will constantly be observed and judged by your troops. They want to know what kind of leader they are following. A single decision can make or break your reputation. Yes, they will always listen to your orders and follow your commands because of the rank and authority you hold. But the aim is to make them voluntarily and respectfully follow your commands and orders.'

Deepak was nodding along. Once Deo stopped, he asked, 'But, sir, what do you do when you have to bend the rules to help someone? To give you an example, one of our boys had an emergency at home but his allotted leave was over. Should you send him on leave so he can take care of his family or follow the rules and not let him go?'

Deo smiled. 'Good question. I guess Danny sent him on leave, didn't he?' he asked.

Deepak smiled and nodded.

Deo waved and said nonchalantly, 'No one can change Danny! The reason is Danny's own personality and leadership style. There is no formula for being a good leader, but what matters is that you should have your own style which your troops can connect with. Once this understanding is achieved, the troops will know how to work with you effectively. Deepak, become a leader that defines you. Then you will never have to put up an act, and you'll be true to yourself, your team and organization. The charade of trying to be someone else never lasts, and you end up losing respect in every quarter. Be Deepak and no one else.'

Deepak replied with an emphatic, 'Yes, sir.'

'Everyone will fear you for your rank. But people will love you for your human nature as a leader,' Deo continued. Contrary to popular belief, it's empathy and love that makes a great military leader, not ruthlessness and barbarism. You may choose what to love, and love it passionately till your dying breath, but that is where great men have always made a mark for themselves.'

Deo stood up, and as he started to walk out, looked at Deepak and said, 'Now get ready to leave for Dehradun. And always remember your Chetwode Motto.'

Deo was referring to the words of Philip Chetwode, a chief of the British Indian Army whose words have been adopted by the Indian Military Academy as every officer's motto, 'The safety, honour and welfare of your country come first, always and every time. The honour, welfare and comfort of the men you command come next. Your own ease, comfort and safety come last, always and every time.'

'Yes, sir,' Deepak said crisply, even though he was still trying to grasp the significance of Col Deo's words. He planned to call Danny at the hospital and update him on his travel plans. The rest of the conversation he decided to keep to himself and ponder upon.

Deepak went to the adjutant's room and asked for the travel briefing. An adjutant is the point person for a unit's operations, training, movement, discipline and other related issues. Maj Sukhinder Singh had been the adjutant of this unit for almost two years now. Col Deo had immense faith in him and gave him a lot of freedom to run the unit. He called Sukhinder 'Mini Chanakya' and often said if he was to manage a political party, he could ensure its victory all by himself.

Sukhinder was known for his cool head and brilliant analytical mind, which earned him the respect of one and all in the unit. But people also knew he wished he was given field command of a company, so that he could show how good he could be in field operations too. Deepak thought Sukhinder would make an excellent company commander, but needed to speak to the CO about his aspirations.

'Welcome, hero,' Sukhinder said to Deepak, and gestured for him to sit down.

Deepak saluted, sat down and told him the purpose of his visit.

'Of course, I'll get to it. But before that, I have something interesting to share with you. Did you know the guy your company killed was actually one of the most sought-after cipher code experts within all the tanzeems and even the ISI? His name was Mohammad Rasool Bhat and he had been on everyone's radar for a long time. He was the one responsible for setting up codes, communication and drop points for terrorists, handlers and OGWs. We hit a jackpot in his bag—the Intelligence and SIGINT (Signals Intelligence) guys are having a party at Corps HQ. So, congratulations and well done once again,' Sukhinder said, standing up and extending his hand.

Deepak jumped from his chair and shook his hand. 'Sir, do we also get to see the contents of his backpack?' he asked while sitting down again.

'Technically, we are supposed to send everything to the intelligence guys at HQ. They go through the material and share relevant details with formations and units. On a very "need to know" basis. But since we are the kings of the jungle and always have first access to every recovery, we always make photocopies of everything to review at our end. Very "we need to know" basis,' Sukhinder replied, grinning and using air quotes to highlight the joke.

Deepak smiled and asked if he could see those copies. Sukhinder asked him to come to the operations room after dinner. 'Right now, our analysis team is working on them with the CO,' he explained.

They discussed Deepak's travel plans. In fact, they kept talking almost till dinner time. Deepak realized how much he still had to learn, and how life in the Army was not just about finding and killing terrorists. An officer was responsible for a million other things in life, and he promised himself he would spend more time with Sukhinder and learn as much as possible.

After his discussion with the adjutant, he went to his room and dialled the number for the Base Hospital to talk to Danny. He had a lot of updates for him now.

16

Danny only got back to his senses a couple of days after the encounter in the village. The doctors had to perform a minor surgery on him and he was kept under anesthesia for a day. Once out of his drug-induced stupor, Danny felt much better and lively, and he decided to enjoy his break at the hospital—he thought of it as a luxury resort where you got good food, TV and internet, staff fawning over you, pretty nurses and doctors walking around, and for what it was worth, no terrorists. The Srinagar Badami Bagh cantonment was one of the most guarded places in the Kashmir Valley, and Danny never understood why anyone would feel unsafe or paranoid in the hospital. 'I'm not paranoid, 'The fine line between caution and paranoia is where effective security plans are made,' he used to say in the unit when people criticized him for his emphasis on safety.

Danny decided he would not do anything that would raise hackles here. He planned to just relax, enjoy the break and not stress about anything. But on the third day of having gained consciousness, he was ready to lose consciousness again. Capt Rupali, a dusky damsel with jet black thick hair and doe eyes, came to check on him as part of her morning rounds. Danny had no guard against this offensive. He could barely speak when she asked him about his condition. He just kept mumbling, and she thought he was still delirious due to the anaesthesia. She took some notes, wished him a speedy recovery and turned to leave his room. That's when Danny blurted out instinctively, 'When will you come again?'

She turned back with a quizzical look. 'Sir? I didn't understand. Do you need something?'

'Umm, no. But I was just asking when you will come by next, so that I can prepare some points to discuss with you,' Danny said, trying his best to keep the conversation casual. But even he realized how lame he sounded.

'Sir, Dr Ramalingam is on duty later today. He will be taking his rounds around 4 p.m. so you can share all your points with him. I have made the notes for him in your file,' Capt Rupali explained.

They send a flower in the morning, and in the evening, they'll send a thorn! Danny thought, and grimaced.

'But isn't it better that one doctor handles a patient, so the progress can be monitored effectively?' Danny asked, trying again not to sound desperate.

'Oh, sir, then I can hand over the file to Dr Ramalingam and request him to visit you in the morning too. You are originally his patient,' she said, a tad disappointedly.

Fuck, fuck, fuck—the word was now pounding in Danny's head.

'Actually, don't pay attention to my thoughts. It is probably better that multiple doctors look after a patient.

You know, if someone misses out something, the other one can notice that. That's a better format, I think,' he said, now trying to salvage the situation.

'Of course, sir. Then I will see you tomorrow morning. Have a nice day, sir. Jai Hind!' she said and left.

Danny slumped back into his bed and said to himself, 'Grow up, man, grow up.'

He spent the rest of the day trying not to think about Capt Rupali, but the more he tried, the more he thought about her. It had been years since someone had made him feel like a teenager. After a couple of failed early romances, he had decided he was meant only to hunt terrorists in the jungle and should not even try his luck with women. Danny's was a handsome face with a hint of north-eastern features. He stood reasonably tall at five foot ten, and had a solid, athletic body. He spoke very well, had a baritone and was a good-natured human being. Women were often interested in talking to him, but he just wasn't interested in following up and taking things forward. The woman he had truly loved with all his heart had left him a few years back. He was a passionate man, so it took him a long time to get over her. Maybe he still hadn't.

But this, Danny thought, was different. Capt Rupali was different. He just didn't know what to do or say. It was a very complicated situation—him being the patient and she his doctor. The fact that they were both in the Army was not going to make things easier either. But he decided he would not give up easily.

In the evening, Danny paid the orderly to get him a nice deodorant and hair gel from the shopping complex. He called the barber for a haircut. He went to the library in his wheelchair and got a couple of books—who knows, she might be a reader and that could be a conversation starter. He was laying the ground for the meeting with her the next morning. 'If only it were as easy as killing terrorists,' he thought to himself as he placed the books on his side table at an angle so that the person standing in front could see them.

Morning came and Danny brushed, shaved and washed himself with vigour, applied the hair gel, combed his hair to perfection, and drowned himself in the deodorant. Whatever best he could manage with his limited mobility, he did it all. He placed himself on the bed neatly and waited. When he heard a commotion in the corridor, he knew the doctors were on their rounds. He immediately picked up a book and started reading.

Rupali entered his room and started coughing violently. Danny panicked. 'What happened? Are you okay?' he asked as she ran outside. After a few seconds, a nurse came in and opened all the windows. Rupali walked in a little later and, still coughing a little, said, 'I'm sorry, sir. I am allergic to deodorants and perfumes and your room is full of it.'

Danny's face went red. 'I'm so sorry. I was just trying to take the edge off the hospital smell. I'll take care from tomorrow,' he said.

'It's okay. I'm all right now. How are you feeling? Any pain or dizziness?' she replied calmly, getting back to business.

'No, I'm all good. Everything normal. Got some books from the library to pass my time here. Do you read? What's your favourite genre?' Danny said, trying to be charming.

'Are you going to the bathroom regularly? Have you been able to pass stool? I can organize an enema—patients who are under anaesthesia for long end up with severe constipation. If you need some help, please let me know,' Rupali replied without even looking up from her file and ignoring his question about books.

Danny got even more red-faced and embarrassed. I'm trying to woo her and she is asking about shit and piss. 'What is wrong with her,' he thought.

'I'm okay. Everything is normal. Don't think I need any help in that department,' he said hurriedly, figuring this was the simplest way to close this particular conversation.

'Then it's good, sir. Also, I will be starting another course of medication for you. The nurse will give you a couple of medicines right after lunch, just letting you know. Anything else you need?' she asked.

'No, I'm good. What else could I need?' Danny said with a weak smile. He knew when it was time to wrap up an operation—no point sitting in ambush when the terrorists had passed.

'Right sir, get well soon. Jai Hind!' Rupali said, then saluted and left.

Danny heaved a big sigh and watched her leave.

Suddenly, she came back and said, 'By the way, sir, I spoke to Major Ramalingam, and from now on, I'll visit you in the evening too. I want to learn more about your kind of injury, so I will be your treating doctor now. In case you need to talk to me, I am at extension 2297 during the day. You can call directly from your phone. It's 2297. You have a nice day, Major Danny.' And she gave a smile and left.

'Target in the kill zone! Ready your weapons, boys,' Danny thought to himself, smiled and fell back into his bed.

'2297. 2297. 2297,' he kept repeating long after she had gone, with a mischievous smile on his face.

17

Deepak called Danny late night with the news the adjutant had shared—about the terrorist killed in the village being a code master. Danny got really excited and asked him to gather more intel. Meanwhile, he decided to try and get out of the hospital as fast as possible.

However, it was not to be so. Military doctors deal with such enthusiasm to return to the frontlines everyday, and they've learnt to make sure that the injured get the requisite rest and care. Danny's request for an early discharge was denied, and when he had spent a few more days in the hospital, he was informed that after another week or so, he was to be sent on mandatory sick leave for four weeks. This made him really mad.

The only thing that provided a relief from his otherwise frustrated state of mind was focussing on the details of the operation. He tried to connect the dots on whatever had happened in the past couple of weeks. He knew the code master never travelled alone—his presence in the village meant there were more bad guys roaming around, and somehow, he had been left behind or separated from the group and had to take shelter in the village, where he got killed.

The operation in which Danny, Deepak and their team had neutralized the group of five terrorists passing through their area had been just a few days ago. Then, there was that IED blast close to their unit's gate, in which two bodies had been found. Why would a suicide attack require two people in the car? Why was there suddenly so much movement in their area? What was the code master, who should ideally be in some cosy hideout in a city, doing running around with a group in the jungles?

He could sense that something was up, but could not figure out what. So, he decided to talk to his friend and coursemate from the NDA, Maj Pratyush Atri, who was posted in the military intelligence (MI) unit in Srinagar. The MI collated inputs from all over the corps zone and always had a much bigger and clearer picture.

He dialled the military exchange from his room and asked to be connected to Maj Atri. A couple of minutes and different ringtones later, Atri picked up and said, 'Hello, Danny?'

On military phones, identities are always disclosed to the receiver, so this was Atri looking for confirmation that it was indeed his old friend on the line.

'Ha ha, yes, yes! Danny here, my boy. How are you doing, man? I'm in Srinagar Base Hospital enjoying the hospitality of the Medical Corps,' Danny said, delighted to talk to him after years.

Atri sounded equally excited. 'I know, brother, I know. I just got back from Baramulla fifteen minutes ago. I heard about you getting shot, but I was in an operation so I couldn't contact you. I was actually going to visit you next week, because I've got to leave for Udhampur right now for a command planning conference. But, good that you called. How are you feeling? Getting better? Are the nurses cute? Anyone giving you sponge baths?'

Atri guffawed, as he always tended to do. Danny laughed at this rapid-fire burst of questions and then decided to come to the point, 'You are still the same idiot you always were. Anyway, I am much better and should be back in action soon. But I need to meet you urgently. So, let's meet as soon as we can.'

'Sure, I was coming anyway. I'll see you next week. Just stay where you are and don't go running around the hills,' said Atri, sensing the urgency in Danny's voice.

'Sounds good. You attend your conference and let's talk next week in detail,' said Danny.

'Sure thing, buddy. See you soon. You also take your pills and be a good boy.' Atri's sarcasm had an undertone of care.

Danny hung up and lay down on his bed, and began making mental notes about the points he wanted to discuss with Atri. If someone could help him get some insight into what was happening, it would be this old buddy.

18

Once Nar Bahadur Thapa's coffin was loaded into the airplane, Lt Deepak and Subedar Ram Bahadur took their place as passengers. The liaison officer (LO) at Srinagar airport was of great help in dealing with the airline and airport authorities, and after they had boarded, Ram Bahadur went over the procedure with Deepak, explaining their responsibilities and duties once they reach their fallen teammate's house.

During the flight, the pilot announced to the passengers that they were carrying the mortal remains of a brave soldier of the Indian Army, at which a few youngsters shouted slogans like 'Long live India' and 'Long live Indian Army'. But some elite-looking people on the flight rolled their eyes. Deepak realized that he was out in the real world, where not everyone held the olive green in the same regard. Since both he and Subedar Ram Bahadur were in civilian clothes, nobody knew that they were accompanying the body. It was like witnessing the world in disguise.

The flight was fairly short, and they landed in Dehradun before noon. Nar Bahadur Thapa's village was around thirty kilometres from the airport. The local unit had sent a few vehicles and some men in ceremonial dress to accompany the mortal remains to the village. Both Deepak and Ram Bahadur changed into uniform at the airport and got into the car sent for them. An open truck, covered in garlands, was to carry the coffin. The coffin was placed in the vehicle and a couple of soldiers sat next to it, and thus started the journey towards Thapa's village.

Around two kilometres from the village, Deepak started to notice large crowds on both sides of the road. Hoardings and banners carrying images of Nar Bahadur and slogans such as 'Long live Nar Bahadur' were on display. People were throwing flowers and garlands on the vehicle carrying the mortal remains of Thapa. As Deepak's car made its way, the vehicles standing on the road came to life and started following them. Deepak was getting tense at seeing such a large crowd. He looked at Subedar Ram, who was calmly looking outside the window. As if he sensed Deepak looking at him, Ram turned his head and saw the youngster's stressed face. He patted Deepak's leg and said, 'Sir, don't worry. All these people from neighbouring villages and cities have come to pay their respects. There will be thousands of people. The local unit would have organized a guard of honour. You and I have to focus only on the family and our part of the procedure. It can be very overwhelming, so do not hesitate to ask me if anything is bothering you.'

'Thanks, Ram saab. I'm glad you are here with me,' Deepak said, reassuring the subedar as well as himself. Then he went back to observing the size and fervour of the crowd on the road.

They reached Thapa's village within a few minutes, and Deepak noticed a team of men from another Gorkha unit, with a band, waiting adjacent to a house. This must be the guard of honour and the ceremonial band from the local unit in Dehradun, he thought. He was glad to find they were Gorkhas too. It was always comfortable to deal with your own.

Once the vehicles stopped, the commander of the team, Subedar Bal Singh Tamang, a stocky and sharp-looking Gorkha, walked up to Deepak and gave a crisp salute. His entire team was in ceremonials, with proper Gorkha hats and khukris on display. Ram Bahadur and Bal Singh discussed coordination and procedure, while Deepak started looking at the truck from which Thapa's coffin was being removed.

The whole world came to a standstill for Deepak when he heard the wailing cries of Thapa's family and friends. It was surreal how thousands of people were chanting Nar Bahadur's name—the whole village was packed with humans, high on adrenaline and national pride. One group was shouting 'Long live India', while another group was singing a famous patriotic song from an old Bollywood movie. As the Gorkha team carried the coffin on their shoulders towards Thapa's house, people threw flowers, garlands and even Holi-like colours on it. Deepak hurried to join the team, as he and Ram needed to be present when they reached the family.

As Deepak made his way through the crowd, he kept checking if Ram was following him. The deafening noise from the crowd, the endless pats on the back, the local youngsters who were making a path for him through the crowd and holding his hand to guide him, the loud crying— the atmosphere sent Deepak into a trance where he just kept moving, step after step after step. He had never been in such a situation. He had never even been to a cremation, so his young mind was still coming to terms with the magnitude of this ceremony.

As he pushed and shoved through the crowd, Deepak suddenly found himself in a small courtyard. He followed the troops carrying the coffin inside the house and was sure he would never forget the sight till his dying day. Thapa's family was distraught, crying their hearts out as they saw the coffin being placed on the ground. He immediately realized who the mother was as she broke free from the group and hugged the coffin. Her dishevelled hair, crushed clothes and puffed eyes told the story of a woman who had lost everything. She kept hugging the coffin and banging her head and fists on it; nobody in the room had the strength to even move a step and pull her back.

For Deepak, the noise outside seemed to have been muted. Time itself felt like it had stopped, and he seemed to be having an out-of-body experience where he was just watching this tide of grief from far away. Some women and a man, possibly Thapa's father, finally stepped forward and got the mother to step back from the coffin. Subedar Ram went forward and started asking everyone to step back, as they were about to open the coffin.

It was time for the family to see the face of their loved one for the last time, as the body would be removed from the coffin and placed on the ground for rituals.

Ram then removed the national flag from the top of the coffin and started folding it in a crisp military drill with the help of others. Someone came to Deepak, shook hands with him and started talking. Deepak had no idea what he was saying—the words didn't make sense and his face was a blur. It was then that Deepak realized that even his own eyes were misty. How can your heart not break on seeing a mother in this state? The lid of the coffin was removed, and Deepak noticed that Thapa's body was wrapped in a white cloth. His young face was ashen white, with two cotton swabs placed in his nostrils. Just a couple of days ago, he had been chatting with Deepak, and had been so full of life and energy. It felt like he might just get up again and start cracking his usual jokes. But that was not to be.

As the body was moved to the ground in order for the family and others to pay their respects and for religious ceremonies, Deepak heard another sharp cry from Thapa's mother. She was beyond consoling now as she leapt forward and hugged the body, kissing the ashen face again and again. She just sat down on the floor, kept his head on her lap and started talking to him. Nobody knew what to tell the mother of this young soldier, who had left many dreams and promises unfulfilled. Nar Bahadur had been her only son and she did not want to believe that he wasn't there anymore. She kept running her hands through his hair and touching his face, as if she was trying to relive every moment she had spent with him, watching him grow from a baby into a strapping young man. She was talking as though she were having a conversation with him, and expected him to reply.

It suddenly hit Deepak—this could've been his own mother, and that body could have been him. The scene wouldn't have been much different. He could not imagine making his mother go through this; he could not fathom giving her so much pain and anguish. He would die before seeing her in this state. But wasn't that exactly what Thapa had also done? How ironic life can be.

A tap on his arm snapped him back into the moment— Subedar Ram told him they had to talk to the father. Deepak followed him to a room inside the small house and found a man sitting with his head in his hands and sobbing. Ram tapped him on his shoulder and as he looked up through his tear-soaked red eyes, Ram introduced Deepak as Nar Bahadur's officer and the last person to see him alive. Deepak leaned forward, took the father's extended hand in both of his and sat down next to him. The man broke down, hugged Deepak and started bawling again. Deepak put his arm around his shoulders. 'Mr Thapa, Nar Bahadur was one of the bravest soldiers in our unit. He gave his life saving the lives of his mates. We are all very proud of him, and please remember, we are your family too,' he said and looked at Ram, who gave a small nod of approval.

Thapa's father gathered himself, poured some water into a glass and drank a big gulp. To Deepak, he looked bereft of any energy or life. 'Sir, thank you for your words. But in the end, it is only us who have lost everything. The world will move on, the unit will move on, the Army will move on. In some time, the local MLA and DC are coming. They will make a show of putting some flowers. Tomorrow, they won't even remember who Narey was, or who we, his family, are. The child we loved and nurtured has been taken away from us, and we have decades and decades of loneliness ahead of us, unless this grief kills us sooner. Did you see his mother? How do I tell her that everything will be all right? After today, it never will,' Thapa's father said.

Deepak had a lump in his throat and decided against even trying to speak.

Ram also sat next to Thapa's father and started talking in chaste Gorkhali. Deepak had still not perfected the language and only caught a few words. Ram was trying his best to console him. He also handed over an envelope from the unit with all the essential documents which the family would need to process financial claims.

They spent a few more minutes in the room, and Ram told Deepak they should give the family some time. They both shook hands with the sobbing father and left the room.

By now, a few relatives had taken Thapa's mother to another room, and some others were taking the body to prepare it for the last rites. The whole house had a gloomy, lifeless feel to it. It seemed as though breath had been sucked out of the very walls and left them with a desperate gasp. The crowd outside was shouting slogans that did nothing to pacify the family. Deepak did not doubt their motivation and patriotism, but at this point, even the grand gestures of committed euphoric crowds, chanting praises, seemed like they were not enough. It felt like nothing could do justice to the death of a brave soldier. This was the first time he was dealing with the death of someone he had been close to. And the irony was that he had no right to cry or beat his chest like the others. He had to stand straight and continue to give the impression of being tough and pragmatic like the organization he belonged to, the Indian Army. He needed to be an anchor today, not a bobbing ship without sails ready to be blown in any direction by the winds of dejection and melancholy.

Deepak moved into the courtyard, which had been barricaded by the Dehradun troops, away from the physical reach of the crowds. By now, he had conditioned himself to drown out the cries. Someone offered him a chair, and he just slumped into it.

The contrast of real death versus the notional sacrifices represented in slogans and songs was very evident to Deepak now. He had started to understand why soldiers were the way they were. He felt as though his mind had evolved at the speed of light He knew what it meant when a soldier asked for leave or worried about his family back home. Deepak realized why Maj Danny, Col Deo and other seniors in the unit made decisions the way they did—they had been through all this and more. These experiences were rites of passage in becoming a man and an officer, and he clenched his fist with resolve. 'Never again,' he said to himself. He would ensure that no soldier or family ever had to go through this trauma as long as he was serving. He would always keep their safety ahead of anything else. This, he realized, was his biggest learning today.

Soon, the body was carried out on a stretcher, covered with the national flag and carried by Subedar Ram and three soldiers of the local unit. Following it were the bereaved family members, friends and the Pandit ji of the village. In that crowd, Deepak's eyes again found Thapa's mother, who was barely in a condition to walk and was being helped and supported by other women. 'How do you gather the strength to take this walk,' he thought to himself.

He continued walking behind the pallbearers with the Gorkha contingent. The crowd was in a frenzy now, with thousands of people shouting 'Bharat Mata ki Jai' at the top of their voices. The residents of every house they passed threw flowers at the procession. They joined their hands and bowed their heads. But when Deepak noticed the pride that was mixed with sorrow that the whole village and the people who had come from neighbouring villages showed, his melancholic mood started to get better. He looked up to the sky and sent a silent prayer—'Die I will if I have to, Mother. But the death will be so glorious that the whole world will salute you that day!'

They finally reached the cremation ground. The band and the party that would be performing the gun salutes took their positions. As Nar Bahadur's body was laid on the pyre, the soldiers removed the Tricolour—the biggest honour anyone could wear on his body—in a quick, neat procedure, folded it nicely and handed it over to Deepak, who went to Thapa's father and presented it to him. The father took it with shaking hands and immediately buried his face in it, crying uncontrollably. Deepak hugged him and took him to the side. After consoling him, Deepak went back and laid a wreath on the pyre on behalf of the entire unit. Subedar Bal Singh Tamang placed the wreath from the Dehradun division commander's side. Deepak, Ram Bahadur and Bal Singh laid a few more wreaths on behalf of the Army chief, the Northern Command, the 15 Corps, etc., and then, family and friends went to the pyre and paid their last respects. Deepak just could not bear to see the parents hugging their son's body for the last time before they were led away. Ram gave the signal to Pandit ji to proceed.

The Gorkha band played the bugle and the firing team let out volleys of blank rounds from the INSAS rifles on their shoulders. The crowd was absolutely silent, observing with awe and pride. Nar Bahadur, their local hero, was today a national hero deserving of this honour. After the rituals were completed, the father was called to light the pyre, which he did with hands shaking, crying his heart out.

Ram came to Deepak and said, 'Sir, we can leave.'

Deepak nodded, and went forward to meet the father again. He hugged him and shook his hands and told him to call if he needed any help. He thought for a second and decided to meet the mother too. He went to her and touched her feet; she held his shoulders, hugged him tight and started crying again. He could feel her pain through her tears. He didn't move a muscle and let her cry, for he knew what that mother had lost. When she was too tired to cry anymore, she moved back, kept her hand on his head and said, 'You take care of yourself, son. He is not coming back, but I do not want any more of you going that way. God bless you, my son.'

And she just turned and walked away to her relatives.

* * *

When Deepak and Ram left the village, a lot of locals came and shook hands with them, and children saluted them all the way out. Both of them thanked Subcdar Bal Singh Tamang for his help, and got into their car and started for Dehradun. Deepak was staying in a guest room there that night. The next day, they had a flight back to Srinagar.

Later that night, Deepak called his mother and talked to her for a while. She was ecstatic to hear his voice after so long, and also pleased that he seemed enthusiastic to share details about his life. He went to bed thinking about his resolve—that he would never let any other parent suffer like this under his command.

19

Danny and Rupali soon became good friends. She would always spend an extra few minutes with him during her rounds in the morning and evening, and would sometimes even drop by during the day. Danny would also call her on the phone, and they would chat.

Danny found a certain comfort in talking to Rupali. She had an easy-going personality and laughed often. She would ask about his life in operations, and he would tell her the most subdued version of it. She understood well that he was like a caged tiger right now, raring to get back to his jungle. She gave him all the advice she could on how to take care of the injury, and related medical advice. However, they both realized pretty soon that their relationship was not going to be romantic, mostly because of the difference in the way they understood relationships. Somehow, they never clicked that way. Rupali was at a point in life where she was looking to get married and Danny had no such intentions. She also sensed that he hadn't got over his previous girlfriend. It could have been these reasons or some other, but both of them changed gears almost simultaneously.

One night while talking to her mother, who had always encouraged Rupali to find someone for herself, she tried to describe Danny and why he was not the right person for her. She told her mother that Danny lived in extremes. There was nothing grey for him. The world, in all its versions, existed only in black and white. He could go to any extent to save the lives of others, but there was no guarantee of whether he would care to save his own. He didn't think of the future. For him, life was what it was today. He was not like normal men who thought of buying a house, building a bank balance and planning for the future. His mind and body were like arrows focused only on killing terrorists and nothing else. How could she think of having a stable relationship with someone like that?

At one point during their initial conversations, which were borderline flirtatious and hinted at progressing towards something more than just friendship, they both realized that the frame they were trying to fit each other in did not match with the picture they had in mind. Danny somehow kept looking for the love he had lost in Rupali and Rupali was looking for someone with more stability in thoughts and life. And so, they had an honest discussion which ended in a handshake and a hug and both were happy to have found a good friend in each other.

They continued to enjoy each other's company and liked the way their friendship was getting cemented. In spite of their different approaches towards life, they found a dependable and honest friend in each other. In fact, once the possibility of romance and a relationship was out of the way, they found it easier to talk to each other and bring forth their real selves undauntingly.

Almost a week had passed, and Danny was much better. He could walk around now and had started his physiotherapy exercises. He was sure that within another week he would be back in his unit.

However, during her morning rounds, Rupali told Danny that he would be sent on medical leave in some time, and that he should book his air tickets and take care of other formalities.

She knew he wasn't too happy to hear that and so, she gave him a chocolate to try and make up for the not-so-happy news. 'Will this cheer you up?' she asked with a smile.

'Really appreciate the sugar overload. But I wish you could've given me the discharge slip instead,' Danny replied with a smile.

'Oh Major, Major, Major, you should enjoy life a little. Take a break from the jungle-bashing. Go home, relax, give your leg some rest and come back stronger. I can assure you, limping around in the jungle is not going to help you in operations,' she said, while writing something in her file.

'Maybe you are right. Anyway, thanks for the chocolate.' He raised the chocolate to his forehead to give her a salute with it.

After talking for a few more minutes, Rupali left to continue her rounds. Danny switched on the TV. The local news was only talking about the home minister's upcoming visit to Srinagar. Politicians and anchors were shouting over each other, as though trying to win some decibel match!

Danny kept surfing through the channels but didn't find anything interesting.

He had just switched off the TV when his buddy, Maj Atri, walked in. A stocky man with thinning hair and an endearing smile enveloped in a beard, Maj Pratyush Atri entered wearing a grey pheran, carrying a worn-down laptop bag on his left shoulder. He barely looked like an Army officer.

Atri ran to hug Danny. After a lot of 'how you doing?' and back-slapping and mutual insults, Atri pulled up a chair, sat down, put his feet up on Danny's bed and asked, 'Can we smoke here?'

Danny laughed and nodded. 'Sure, go ahead. Maybe they will throw me out on grounds of discipline and I will get discharged early,' he said, only half-joking.

After all the jokes were over, Atri began in a serious tone, 'So, tell me, Mr Danny … what can I do for you? What can a lowly intelligence major do for the legendary Danny Deka, the terror of terrorists in Kupwara?'

Danny looked at him seriously and spoke very softly, not wanting to let his words go beyond the door. 'We killed Mohammad Rasool Bhat a few days ago. The Code Man. He was loitering around deep in Kupwara, and we caught him alone in a village. The week before that, we neutralized a track of five in our area. All of them had new and very good equipment and clothing. The day we killed Code Man, an IED blew up near our unit's gate. There were two men inside the car carrying the explosives. Not one, but two. So, you tell me what's going on. Why these sudden movements? What is happening?'

Atri, who was listening intently so far, took a deep breath and rested his head on the chair. He then leaned forward with elbows on his knees, opened his mouth to speak, halted and finally asked, 'Stays between us?'

Danny nodded. 'Of course.'

Atri nodded slowly and took another deep breath. 'Listen, DD, what I can tell you is that something big is coming. We don't know what because we have not been able to figure it out. But the activities in your area are not isolated. The RR also bumped off three in Baramulla, and I went to see the documents recovered from the site. These documents were same as the one you have found during your search mission. It is a strange document, which we have not been able to understand so far. But they match letter to letter and number to number. Here, have a look, I got you a photocopy. I knew your next question would be, "Can I see it?"' He reached into his bag and took out a couple of sheets stapled together. Danny started scanning them—they just had some illegible text and a few random letters and numbers thrown in some order. There was nothing that made any sense—no heading, no signature, no logos or images to suggest any lead into solving the code.

Danny went through the pages again, shook his head in exasperation and said, 'This doesn't make any sense to me. Did your guys have a look at it?'

'Of course, and we couldn't crack the code. But one thing is obvious. A few teams of terrorists are moving around with this document. It must be some sort of plan and directions,' replied Atri. 'Now, all these groups are trying to achieve something, either independently or together. But what? That's one of the biggest questions. To tell you the truth, we had no idea about any of it till you killed Code Man Bhat. What we recovered from him gave us a major breakthrough. We still do not understand the document, but we are one step ahead of where we were. Code Man was on his way back from the Muzaffarabad camp via Tangdhar and Kupwara. He was travelling with a group of six and was supposed to reach Srinagar. But I guess something happened when he was around your camp in Panzgam—he got separated and you killed him. We came to know all this from a map and the travel plans he was carrying. Surprisingly, these were in plain text. But even he had a copy of this damned confounding document. We were hoping that since he was the cypher guy, he would have had a key on him for decryption. But nothing.' Atri shrugged and leaned back in his chair.

'All this points towards a major operation being planned,' Danny said. 'If Code Man was specially called to Pakistan for a briefing and was coming back with directions, it definitely means something big is coming. I think both groups that got killed—by us and RR—had met him somewhere near Tangdhar and were getting back from the meeting, moving towards Srinagar. I am sure there are more copies of that document with other groups. He handed them to these guys in person. What I still don't get is that if he could give directions in person, what was the need to give this encrypted document?' Danny pointed towards the document

'That's the million-dollar question!' Atri exclaimed.

Both sat in silence for a few minutes, and then Danny suddenly shouted in excitement, 'Got it! Code Man was called for a briefing because he was in touch with all the groups operating in Kashmir. So, he was briefed by the ISI guys to be the control station. However, at this stage, they did not want to share the details of the operation with the guys who were going to carry it out. What if someone got caught by the Indian Army and revealed the big plan during interrogation? So, Code Man called all of them, told them they were going to be part of this big operation, and gave them this document. Most probably, this was the preparation phase. But they will be given the decryption key to understand the directions only once they are done with their preparations. Right? What do you think?'

Atri gave a two-finger salute, smiled and said, 'Smart thinking, but this theory has a major flaw—how would these guys prepare for an operation without knowing what it is?'

Army officers know that to prepare for any operation, even terrorists need a plan, time and resources. The plan is provided by the leaders and commanders of the tanzeems, while resources like guns and explosives are collected from a designated location and person. All this requires a lot of coordination between the ISI, terrorists and their local supporters. Danny and Atri knew this supply chain very well. What they also knew was that unless you got hold of some good intelligence, it was near-impossible to know about any terrorist action in the future. In this case, they were lucky to have chanced upon a great input, and if they did not act on time, there was no telling what disaster awaited.

'I don't think that's a problem,' said Danny, now gesturing with his hands. 'They can be asked to gather weapons, people and explosives as of now. I doubt anyone can object to it if that's how their hierarchy wants to play it. It is the preparation stage, and we do not know how long it will last. Maybe we have to figure it out before they move stuff to the locations. The thing we have to focus on—'

'Wait, hold on,' Atri interrupted. 'You said this could be the phase where they are moving men and material. So, all these groups who gathered for the meeting with the Code Man are moving to the location. One got killed by you, another by RR. Is it possible that the car that exploded outside your unit was carrying explosives for the same operation? The route is the same, it falls within the right timeline, and it was definitely not an attack on your camp. You guys reacted like it was an attack, but I think it was an accident. There were two guys in the car. Why would two men want to blow themselves up doing the simple task of driving a car to your gate? Plus, they were actually a little far away from your gate, on the main road, with the car facing away from your gate. I think not only men, but even explosives are being moved towards Srinagar. These explosives could have been smuggled through the same route that Code Man came back on after his meeting in Pakistan.'

Atri was on to something, and Danny nodded furiously. 'Bingo! So, let's summarize what we know. Code Man was called to Pakistan to have a coordination meeting for a major attack in Srinagar. He gathered various groups and briefed them without giving exact details. These terrorists were to reach Srinagar and some teams would carry explosives. One such team, which may or may not have been there for the meeting with Code Man, blew itself up due to some fuck-up we might never know about. Two groups have been killed by us and RR. But even now, there are other groups of terrorists converging on Srinagar, carrying encrypted instructions and plans. Did I miss anything?'

Atri shook his head. 'No, covered it all. But now we know what a mammoth problem we have ahead of us. And I have no idea what to do next. Personally, I think the answer lies in finding the person who has the decryption key. Everyone will converge on him to make this operation happen. And I am sure it must be some OGW in Srinagar. But the city is full of them—thousands and thousands. How do we find the right guy?' he asked.

Both were thinking hard and discussed a couple more points, but could not arrive at anything substantial. It was almost lunchtime and Atri had to leave for a meeting, so they decided to give it more thought and meet at the same time the next day to discuss it further.

Atri was about to leave when he looked at Danny and said, 'Would you like to have a look at the material we got from Code Man's haversack? You are one of the best at understanding terrorist operations, so maybe you can see something that we missed.'

'Oh sure, send it to me. I have nothing to do here. Let me have a look and we can discuss it tomorrow,' said Danny, more than happy at the prospect.

'Great. I'll get copies sent to you by today evening. Untill that time, you take care and get some rest. By the way, do you know that there is no guarantee that the promised seventy-two virgins in heaven will be female? So, think about the plight of the poor dead terrorists when you sleep tonight.' Atri said. Both he and Danny laughed and bade each other farewell.

Danny changed his clothes and left for the Mess hall at the Base Hospital for lunch. In his mind, he was sure that the answer to all this was with the person holding the decryption key in Srinagar.

'One key to rule them all!' he said to himself, chuckling.

20

As promised, Atri got the documents sent over to Danny by that evening. Danny was looking at them during the next morning, when Atri entered the room and asked, 'So how are you, my Assamese beauty?'

Danny looked up and smiled. 'All good. Been working on this, but no progress, sorry,' he said and pushed the documents aside forcefully.

'Wow, she is not in a good mood,' Atri joked, then slumped into a chair and put his feet up on Danny's bed. 'You think it is that easy? If the code was that simple, we would have done it ourselves, infantry boy.'

'Have you thought of talking to Major Dilip Jha? He is the only one who has cracked such codes,' Danny said, lifting the coded page and pointing it towards Atri.

'My CO hates him. He would rather die than ask Jha for help, even though he knows he's the only one who can do this, so my hands are tied,' Atri said with a shrug.

'Ah, the petty egos of tiny men! The organization could do so much better if people didn't confuse ranks with competence and age with maturity. I really feel sad when I see brilliant officers getting slaughtered in their careers because a jackass on top could not appreciate their talents and only expected ass-licking. Your CO, I'm sure, knows the stakes here. But his moronic attitude will make everyone suffer. And what's even sadder is that technically, he has a very good excuse—that he cannot share confidential details with a veteran. But talk about innovation in problem-solving in the intelligence community in the Army. This is what it is!' said Danny, fuming.

'Hey, hey … Calm down buddy, calm down. This one insecure guy doesn't represent the whole Intelligence Corps. I told you he doesn't want to take Jha's help. But that doesn't mean we cannot,' Atri said, a smile on his lips.

'Meaning?'

'I am going to contact Jha and request him to come here. This can be totally unofficial and we just keep it between us,' Atri finished with a wink.

Danny almost jumped up in his bed and said, 'Sounds perfect.'

Atri immediately got up. 'Cool, let me organize this, and the next time I visit you, I will have Major Jha and the decoded page with me. You rest and get your mani-pedi,' he said with a laugh, and left the room.

Danny waved goodbye and lay down, smiling. He was very hopeful that Jha could decode the page. That would tell them what was coming and they could counter it in time. He was itching to get back to action.

He was still thinking when Atri barged back in and said, 'Can you come out for one night? I have a solid source we can talk to, but it'll be good if you come along.'

Danny was surprised. They both knew it was near-impossible to step out of the hospital—duty officers were very strict, and if he went missing, he could face disciplinary action.

'But why do you need me?' Danny asked.

'I will explain that later. Can you or can you not?' Atri asked again, hastily.

'I can try and talk to Rupali. But I am not sure,' Danny said. He was just shooting in the dark.

'Great. Just use your charm and say that you have to meet someone important. Whatever you can think of. I will let you know when we go,' Atri said, walking out without even bothering to hear a reply.

'Typical. Idiot,' Danny said with a grunt. Then, he started thinking of an excuse that would make Rupali let him go out for a night when she was the on-duty medical officer.

It was going to be a tough sell, and Danny knew that.

21

Back from Dehradun, Deepak finally got a chance to go through the photocopied documents that Maj Sukhinder had mentioned—all the material Code Man had been carrying. He was very excited to finally have a look at the stuff, and couldn't have guessed that at the same time, Danny was reviewing them in his hospital bed.

Deepak got himself a thermos full of coffee and sat in the operations room after dinner. He kept his pen and notebook on the side to take notes and started sifting through the material. Thankfully for him, Code Man was a well-educated guy who made notes in English. There was a rumour that Bhat had a master's degree in statistics and mathematics, and was a codebreaker and encryptor par excellence.

Deepak started placing the documents in three piles. The biggest one had irrelevant documents like magazines and religious content. The second pile included content that seemed relevant but needed some deliberation—a few paper notes, Bhat's diary and a couple of maps. In the third pile, he put material he couldn't make head or tail of. This had only one document—the same encrypted one Danny and Atri had been discussing in Srinagar.

The second pile was where Deepak was hoping to find something, so he started with the photocopy of a diary with a lot of handwritten notes. Most of it was poetry and religious verses, plus a few recipes for making different kinds of mutton. Deepak soon realized that the only gold was that coded document in the third pile.

Col Deo, the unit intelligence team and other officers had gone through it, but had been unable to crack it. Deepak was sure there had to be something there. If he could find it, he was sure that the CO would appreciate it a lot. Maybe it would stop everyone from calling him D-Cup.

Deepak started leafing through the pages, hoping to find a pattern. He tried some basic letter and number-replacement tricks, but he realized the code was too advanced for him. Having spent almost an hour, he wasn't closer to solving anything. He decided to consult his sensei.

The ringing phone startled Danny—he answered it and was mildly irritated to find it was Deepak, because he was totally focused on the documents. But when Deepak told him that he was working on the same notes, Danny felt happy and relieved. Deepak wasn't the dumbest cookie in the jar, and it would be nice to discuss a few points with him.

'You know how they create these codes, right? A is replaced by B and B by C, so ABBA becomes BCCB. The secret lies in the logic used to make this key. If you have the key, you can decode the entire message easily,' Danny explained.

'Sir, I know,' Deepak said, rolling his eyes. How dumb did Danny think he was?

'Okay, good. And calm down with that pissy tone. Pay attention here. In computers, the encryption happens automatically after you create a key. But here, it is done manually. It also has to do with the fact that they are scared of the Army and intelligence agencies getting hold of their keys. So, Code Man was known to pass coded messages with different keys all the time, making it impossible to track his communications. Even if you solved one, there was no way of knowing what the logic behind the next one would be. Here too, I am sure that he had created the logic manually. So, we just need to figure out the logic that can lead us to the key,' Danny said, scratching his chin and looking at the pages under his night lamp.

'Yes, sir,' Deepak replied excitedly, staring at the coded document.

Danny fell silent again, thinking hard.

'Sir, maybe if we knew his date of birth, favourite books and writers, places, etc., we could figure something out. Such data could help us a lot,' Deepak weighed in.

'Yes, of course, Deepak. Remember when we all had a threesome and he told us all these details while smoking in bed? Why not dig out those notes?' Danny dished out some cold sarcasm and Deepak went absolutely quiet.

'He will not do something so simple. He is a shrewd and skilled man ... Was, was!' Danny reminded himself.

'Sir, don't we have some specialists in MI who work only on these sorts of things?' Deepak asked pensively.

'Yes, there are some guys who do this pretty well. But I spoke to my coursemate here in the intelligence unit. Even they are lost. There used to be one Major Jha who was the most sought-after man in the entire Army for codes. He was the only one who had cracked Code Man's work a few times. But he left the Army and is not available now,' Danny explained.

'Maybe we can reach out to him? Even if he is retired, he wouldn't mind helping, would he?' asked Deepak, dying to solve the mystery.

'Yeah, that's a possibility. My coursemate is thinking along the same lines. Let's see if they can trace Major Jha and get him to help us. Anyway, you go to sleep. I'll update you tomorrow. Good night,' said Danny, keen to be left alone to do some thinking.

'Sure, sir, good night,' said Deepak, hanging up and going back to staring at the piles of documents. He could not help but wonder about the amount of destruction and hate these pages must contain. The more he thought, the stronger his resolve became to unravel the mystery. But he was standing in front of a wall, which he could neither push down nor bypass. He would have to wait for this ace codebreaker, Maj Jha, to take a shot at it.

22

Rupali entered Danny's room huffing and puffing, and came hurriedly to his bedside. 'What? What happened? Are you okay? The nurse messaged that you wanted to see me urgently,' she said with a bit of impatience.

Danny propped himself on one elbow and smiled casually. 'Hey, cool down. I just said I wanted to see you urgently to discuss something,' he said.

Rupali punched him in the arm and frowned mockingly. She turned around, sat on the only chair in the room and said, 'So what is so urgent that you had to call the duty officer away from her desk?'

'Okay, here it is. I need to get out tonight. And you know that it's kind of not allowed. So, I was hoping that you would, you know, let me out for a few hours? That is, if you are, you know, okay with it?' Danny stammered, looking at the floor all along. He was never comfortable asking favours, especially when it meant putting one of his friends at risk. He generally liked to be on the other side—taking risks for those who mattered to him.

Rupali chuckled softly. 'You know, as you said, "if I am

okay with it". As it would appear, I am not. So, no,' she responded with a laugh and started to leave.

'Wait … wait,' said Danny, sitting up on the bed and speaking excitedly. 'Listen, I am serious. I have something exceptionally urgent to attend to, and you have to let me out tonight. I cannot ask anyone else, so I'm requesting you. Come on, I'll get you some chocolates on my way back.'

Danny gave a lopsided smile and tried to charm her into letting him out.

Rupali looked at him sternly and asked, 'What is it?'

Danny sighed and threw his head back. 'I cannot tell you. It's related to operations.'

He got up from his bed, came towards her chair, and looked at her seriously. 'Rupali, you cannot know. It's confidential,' he said softly. 'But it is very critical that I move out tonight to sort something out. You have to help me. There is a lot at risk.'

Rupali got up from her chair and looked him straight in the eye and replied, 'No, Danny, I cannot take that risk. If you are caught, I will be court-martialled. And I don't even know where you are going. What if you get in trouble there, and something happens to you? How will I justify that? By saying I didn't know you were not in your bed? I cannot admit that I allowed you to leave. As much as it is a risk to your health and safety, it's a massive risk to my career and reputation too. What could possibly be so important? Sorry, Danny, I cannot allow it.'

She just shook her head and looked down at her feet, almost apologetic.

Danny sat back down on his bed and shrugged his shoulders. He looked up at her and said, 'Look here. The thing is that I will leave in the next thirty minutes. Major Atri is coming to pick me up. I told you out of respect for our friendship and…'

Rupali raised her hand to silence him. 'Okay, you can leave. And I will not report it as long as I am on duty, which is till 8 a.m. tomorrow. Out of respect for our friendship, which somehow seems to have run its course, I will ensure that no nurse comes to your room, sir. Have a good night. Jai Hind, sir,' she said, giving him a crisp salute and turning to leave.

Danny jumped from the bed and held her by her forearm. 'Hey, please don't be like that. I don't want to take advantage of our friendship and leave without asking you. Please try to understand. I wouldn't do this if it wasn't absolutely essential,' he said sincerely.

Rupali kept looking into his eyes with an angry scowl. She pushed away his hand from her arm and coldly replied, 'Sir, good night.'

And left.

Danny slapped his forehead lightly and muttered, 'There goes another friendship down the drain. This source better be worth it.'

From his almirah, he took out the small bag that Atri had left him. It contained a tracksuit, cap, 9mm Glock, mobile phone and pocket knife. Danny changed into the track suit and wore the cap, secured the 9mm in his waistband and pocketed the knife. He picked up the mobile phone and messaged Atri, 'At RV in 5.'

Danny left the room still wondering what he could do to make it up to Rupali. He kept losing friends because he never had the social skills to keep these associations going. He needed to change, he told himself, as he stealthily made his way towards the hospital gate.

23

Danny met Atri just outside the hospital gate and jumped into his SUV. None of them said anything, and Atri gunned the SUV out of the cantonment. Atri was in civilian clothes, as were the two men sitting behind him, who were both carrying AKs. Once out on the main road, one of the guys handed an AK to Danny, who accepted it. He removed the magazine and checked it, looked through the sights once and put the magazine back in again. Then, he looked at Atri and asked, 'Where to?'

Without taking his eyes off Srinagar's well-lit roads, Atri said, 'I have a guy. Old source. He's from Handwara, but now works here in the irrigation department. He always has some good inputs and keeps a good eye on the happenings around here. I want to find this mystery guy who is the coordinating point. Maybe he knows something.'

'So, why do you need me? I'm sure you've met him many times earlier too,' Danny said.

Atri gave a slight smile, looked at Danny briefly and then shifted his gaze back to the road. He took out a piece of paper and gave it to him. It was the same coded document. 'I'm going to tell him that you are an intelligence officer from Nepal and you found this there, but it was meant for Srinagar, so you have come to us for help,' he explained.

Danny looked confused. 'How does all this help? I mean I can play the Nepali officer well, but how will it help us?'

'Danny boy, intelligence gathering is a very different game. Each source is different, each input is unique. You have to learn how to handle each guy,' Atri explained. 'But one thing is common to all these guys—they are two-faced, greedy sons of bitches who will happily sell their souls for a few extra bucks. By introducing an international officer, I will show him what a big case this is. Big case means big money, and that will give him a good erection. Now, imagine if I told him you are a Major saab from Kupwara, versus telling him you are the head of Nepal's counterintelligence squad. Understood?'

Danny nodded and patted Atri on the back. 'Good thinking, baby, good thinking!'

Atri laughed. 'Thanks. By the way, were you able to get out easily?'

Danny shrugged. 'Oh yeah, Rupali kind of helped me. But she is really pissed. I'll have to do something to make it up to her.'

Atri grinned. 'You two will have children with beautiful eyes and an obsessive addiction to running around in jungles,' he said.

'Oh shut up, you idiot!' Danny said, but ended up smiling.

They kept chatting for another half an hour, and finally stopped outside a very regular-looking house. Atri looked at Danny and said, 'Ground Zero, my man.'

The other men stayed in the car and moved up to the front seats while Atri and Danny went inside. Atri knocked on the door three times.

A smiling man opened the door almost immediately, and signalled to them to come inside. He had not switched on the light so Danny couldn't have a proper look. He was guiding them with a torch, and took them to a back room, which had its lights on and four chairs placed around a small table. Danny noticed that the man was small and pot-bellied, with a long beard, no moustache and almost no hair on his head. He was wearing some cheap jeans and a collared black t-shirt featuring the logo of an unknown brand. He hardly looked like some master informer, but then isn't that the best way to be one, Danny thought.

Once everyone sat down, Atri spoke first. 'Khan saab, this is Mr Pratap Thapa from Kathmandu. He is head of the counterintelligence department there. Thapa ji, this is Mr Bilawal Khan. He is a true patriot and has helped the Indian Army fight terrorism for a long time. You can trust him and share your problem with him.'

Khan shook Danny's hand with both of his, and said, 'Anything, sir, anything. Please tell me, how can I help?'

Danny took out the coded page from his pocket and laid it on the table. He started speaking in a heavy Nepali accent, which wasn't too difficult for a Gorkha officer like him. 'Mr Khan, our team arrested an ISI operative at Kathmandu airport. He had a ticket to Delhi and onwards to Srinagar. Although he is Nepali by nationality, we think his documents may be fake and he could be from Bangladesh.

We are investigating that. However, we found this coded document on him, and we knew he was coming to deliver this to someone in Srinagar. Talking to Major saab here, we realized they found the same document in New Delhi, Srinagar and Kupwara. Now, it is clear that all these couriers were coming to Srinagar to meet someone senior enough— someone who was coordinating with all of them towards some big operation. We need to find that person and need your help in this.'

Khan was listening intently and kept looking by turns at Danny and Atri. Once Danny finished, he looked at Atri with a questioning stare and raised his eyebrows. Atri leaned forward and said, 'He is right. We found this document in Delhi too. I spoke to headquarters and told them that if there is one person who can solve this international-level operation, it is Mr Bilawal Khan. I told them, if required, we will fly Mr Khan to Delhi and Kathmandu to work closely with the Nepali team also. Now, everything is in your hands. The moment we can identify this mastermind in Srinagar, we can start the joint operation in Kathmandu. I hope you don't mind travelling?'

Atri asked the last question with so much innocence that Danny almost laughed at his theatrics.

Khan was excited. 'Of course, sir. I will go wherever you ask me to,' he replied. 'As for this document, I will try and find out what is going on. There are many big OGWs in Srinagar, as you know well. But most of them are inactive as of now. Only a few are active, but I haven't heard of anyone engaged in any serious operation. But then, it is not like all of them report to me daily. I gather what I can and that is a difficult process. You have to make friends, entertain them, pay them, help them, gain trust. You know how it is, Major saab.'

Atri reached into his bag, took out some bundles of cash and kept them on the table. 'Just some advance for your troubles, Bilawal bhai. We really need this information as soon as possible. Mr Thapa has to return shortly to Nepal. Once we find something, we will take care of you.'

'Oh, come on Major saab, it is not about money. You know I am dedicated to working against terrorism in my state, and I will try my best to find out what is going on here,' Khan said, picking up the bundles and keeping them in a drawer.

'But is there something you could tell us now, Khan saab?' said Danny, getting desperate.

Bilawal Khan ran his hand down his flowing beard, his eyes slanted towards the floor. Then, he looked up and dramatically said, 'Maybe there is. I am not sure if it can help you or not. There is a rumour that a woman who has come recently from the UK to work as a communication consultant for the chief minister's secretariat has very strong opinions on Kashmir and pretty radical Islamic views. She has been meeting all the "right people", if you know what I mean. She is said to be a well-known social media celebrity in the UK, and has been here only for a few months. My sources haven't met her in person because she only deals with the top guys. Her name is Sayema something. I am not sure if it makes sense to you or not, but this is the hottest news in the market right now.'

Danny immediately asked, 'But why is an Englishwoman working here?'

Khan shot back, 'Oh, but she is a native to Kashmir, who is now a British citizen. It's said that she has worked with a lot of British politicians too.'

Danny and Atri looked at each other. They liked the sound of it. A Kashmiri immigrant, now with UK nationality, actively working with the chief minister's office could very well be the ISI conduit they were looking for.

'So, can you find out more about this Sayema for us? We will check her online content ourselves. But we need more than that. Hope you understand,' Atri said.

Atri was one of the best social media analysts that the Army had. His ability to create social media campaigns, analyse enemy activity, connect the dots and plan propaganda was second to none. He was rather happy about getting a chance to deploy his strength.

Khan put his hands out and replied, 'Of course, I will get on to this immediately. My cousin, Dr Henna Mehrotra, is married to a Hindu doctor and works with a medical NGO here. She is connected to these people because they keep coming to her medical camps to show their faces and look concerned. Give me one week and I will get you the details.'

They spoke some more about the situation in the city and politics in general, and then bade goodbye.

Back in the car, Atri said, 'This Sayema-lead looks nice. I can tell you behind her "communication consultant" cover and friendly smile, there will be an evil planner who is ready to destroy this city and the country. Hardcore radicals have only one agenda—the destruction of India.'

'You are so right, my friend. I think this lead should pan out well. Let's check her out on social media and see what she is like. But this can also be a futile wild goose chase and waste our time, something we don't have now,' said Danny.

They reached the hospital around 5 a.m. and Danny went into his room quietly. Now, his thoughts were not only on this new lead, but also on how to make up with Rupali.

He called up the duty station and Rupali picked up.

'I am back. Thanks a lot for your help. You have no idea how important this was,' Danny spoke quickly.

'Apparently not as important as our friendship or my job, which you put at risk by vanishing like this. Anyway, good that you got what you wanted. Good night,' she replied bluntly and hung up.

'Why can't women be more understanding?' Danny said to himself, irritated because somehow he couldn't figure women out—friends or girlfriends. He could never act like the metrosexual, overpleasing guys, nor could he not act like himself. He had come to the conclusion that women swoon over the tough, bad guys in movies and books and detest them in real life. Not that he thought of himself as a bad guy, but he was sure that he was as Alpha as they come. Realizing it would be impossible to change himself now, he decided to sleep it off. But his mind was still galloping around trying to figure out the mystery of Sayema. Why would a famous YouTuber leave the UK and get involved in communication plans in Kashmir, of all places? But he knew very well that someone driven by religious motivation would put everything aside in pursuit of their goals. If this Sayema was a person like that, she was more dangerous than a few hundred terrorists put together. After all, it is the ones who build and power the narratives that control the crowd, not a few men with guns. Sayema had the access and cunningness to exploit that fault line. This needed to be investigated thoroughly.

Danny kept thinking about why the security and intelligence agencies were blind to these developments, and their efforts to fight narrative wars were limited to setting up social media accounts to post motivational quotes and photos of military exercises. He always wondered why, in spite of so much talk about information warfare and social media, nothing happened in India. The online world was full of jingoistic, ill-informed individuals, ranting veterans and psychological operations (psy ops) by Pakistan and China. Somehow, the forces just didn't understand the damage this was doing to the credibility, morale and psyche of India's soldiers, and the nation itself.

He fell asleep wondering if someday, the armed forces would actually work on a communications and narrative strategy, and take a step ahead from just making presentations and posting photographs of generals cutting ribbons or archaic wisdom and motivational quotes.

24

Maj Dilip Jha landed at Srinagar airport and Atri was there to receive him. They got into a civilian car, in which two of Atri's men sat in the front as driver and security. Once inside, Atri gave him some more details on what was going on. Jha kept listening to everything and nodding.

The car snaked through Srinagar's traffic and reached a nondescript house in Hyderpora, between the airport and the Badami Bagh cantonment. Atri's man from the front passenger seat got down first and opened the gate to the compound. The car rolled in and the driver parked it in the porch. As everyone alighted, Jha shook hands with Atri's men and thanked them.

Inside, Jha looked at Atri and said, 'Your budgets seem to have improved. This is a good-looking safe house.'

'That's true, sir,' Atri replied, guiding Jha to his room. 'The pressure to monitor the separatists and tanzeems was too much. We needed a couple of bases around the city. This is one of those new ones, under my detachment, so I thought it would be better for you to stay here than at any hotel. You will find it very comfortable and the cook makes excellent

Kashmiri cuisine. Anything you need, sir, just let the boys know. Two of them stay here permanently—Havildar Gupta and Naik Chandran, both from my unit.'

Jha entered the room and was happy to find three things he liked a lot—a desk with a lamp, a jar of Davidoff dark roast coffee and salted peanuts. He looked at Atri, smiled and bowed his head in gratitude. He placed his backpack on the chair and walked around to look through the windows. After having a good look at his surroundings, he turned back to Atri and said, 'I think I'm good. You can leave the documents with me. Let's meet at dinner?'

'Sounds good, sir. And, again, my sincere thanks to you for coming here,' said Atri, and handed over a bag containing the coded document, a Kashmiri dictionary, a calculator, a couple of notepads, coloured pencils and two pens. When he had created it a few years ago, Jha had simply named it 'Codebreaker's Kit', and that's what military intelligence guys still called it.

Atri stretched his arms straight down, clicked his heels, said goodbye to Jha and left. He had a source to meet in another part of the city.

Jha walked slowly to the electric kettle and poured in some water before switching it on. First things first! He believed in fuelling the body with an adequate amount of black coffee before starting any daunting task. He couldn't help but feel nostalgic about the times he would spend days locked up in the rooms of safe houses trying to break codes. He smiled to himself for getting the opportunity to live that life once again.

25

Jha picked up the coded document and started working on the simplest possibilities. Sometimes, the solution was so simple that no one considered it. In his experience, it was better to try and get these simple ones out of the way before graduating to the more complicated ones.

As a codebreaker, all you need is one small entry into the maze. Experienced codebreakers don't aim to solve the whole thing at once; initially, they look for one flag that would point them in the right direction. For example, a letter appearing more times than others could be a vowel. Two- or three-letter words are generally articles or prepositions like 'on', 'is' or 'the'. From here, you pick up a letter and try to recreate more words. Alphanumeric codes are often a signal that the numbers might indicate the position of letters in the code that make up a word. While images can be a great hint, they can also send you on a wild goose chase.

Thankfully, Jha thought, this code did not have any images or diagrams. Just plain letters and numbers.

The code read,

1. LNMOTM DWBOTMDPLN
    SGFSBOFSDPLNLO

2. DSDPDWMOSG DSLNBSFS
    SGKEPOLNLNMO HWBOLSMO
    DCLNPOBOMOMOBO

3. SGPOBOPOFLFLLO KEBODWHWFLFS
    SLBOKEFSLNDWLB
    SGPOLSLODSMODPHWLSPWSG

4. MNBODWBSFLCB
    NBLNLNTMNBLNDWCOSG
    FSBODWBOCBDPCOPOLSDWTM

    a. DSBOFSFL11120

    b. DSBOFSFL21125

Purely alphabetic codes were the most complicated, according to Jha. Alphanumeric ones generally offered the possibility of working on numbers through some combinations or algorithms, but pure letters were hell to deal with. And this looked like one of them, despite two sets of numbers at the end. Jha realized quickly that these numbers were not part of the code key, but just serial numbers for something—door, building, gate, road or anything that followed serial numbers. He decided to get to it later.

Jha had twice cracked the Code Man's encryption in the past, and thus, knew he did not follow computerized coding mechanisms. This had two advantages for the terrorists.

The first was that Code Man's clientele generally hung around in jungles and mountains, with no access to computers or laptops; even smartphones did not help in this case. Given a key, all the recipients of the coded message could easily translate the message by themselves. So, he believed in making personal, manual keys to write his coded messages, which transformed regular text into something complex like the one he was holding in his hand. He would use some random calculation or trick to replace all the letters and create the key, then use it to write the message.

The second, and bigger, advantage was that even if the code was put through brute force methods in a computer codebreaking software, it was impossible to decipher it because if he had decided to call a grenade an 'aloo' (potato) and an AK a 'mooli' (radish), the computer could keep working till the end of time but couldn't go into this language change-vegetable transformation dimension. So, the code had to be broken manually, and for that, Jha needed to get into the mind of Code Man.

The first time he had broken this guy's code, he had found that he was replacing letters with the initials of Bollywood stars. The next time, it had been the first two letters of twenty-six varieties of spices. He was that random. So, Jha had no idea what weird and incomprehensible technique he had used this time.

Jha then straightened his arms and with both his hands held the document far from himself, and started running his eyes over it. Using this method of 'pattern detection', he was looking for some of the same alphabetic patterns to stand out. He must have stared at it for half an hour, then kept it down, closed his eyes and started thinking. All the 'words' in the code had even numbers of letters. Also, there was a lot of repetition of two-letter sets—this meant each two-letter set represented one letter.

Good going, Jha thought to himself, and after relaxing his eyes for a few minutes, he started working again, trying to figure out the two-letter replacement for a single letter to get at least one word. He worked for almost two hours straight, but got nowhere, so he got up and decided to take a walk to give his mind a much-needed break.

As he was stepping outside, towards the tiny garden, he heard cries of joy and loud clapping in another room. He went inside to check and saw both men from Atri's team sitting comfortably and watching a cricket match—India was thrashing Sri Lanka. Jha stood behind them watching, and his mind went back to his childhood, when he spent most of his afternoons playing his favourite sport at his school ground and getting drenched in sweat. At that time, all he wanted was to become a cricketer and play for India, but pretty soon, he realized he neither had the skills nor the family support needed to pursue this dream. So, he got back to being a good student and focused on college entrance exams.

He was still reminiscing when one of the boys noticed him and immediately shut off the TV and stood up. The other guy followed suit, and both were standing to attention now. Jha waved to them to relax and started enquiring about the match. After a few minutes of conversation on cricket, he decided to get back to his room and continue working. As he walked back to his room, his mind was still on his school ground, and he was smiling to himself, remembering when he would try to copy Sachin Tendulkar as a teenager.

Jha poured himself another coffee, had a smoke and started peering down at the document again, trying to make sense of it. He started picking out evident and repetitive double-letter combos and placed them around as vowels to try and make one word. He just could not. It was very frustrating because now he was starting to worry that the words were not English at all. Maybe they were Urdu or Kashmiri. If that was the case, he would be really screwed. He only had a basic knowledge of these languages, and it would be a near-impossible task to first guess the letter those combinations stood for, and then try to make out a word or a name or location. He held his head in his hands and whispered to the page, 'Come on man, give me some hint.'

He kept trying until Chandran knocked on the door. Jha shouted 'come in' and continued working; the other man entered with a big tray from which came the delicious smell of hot food.

'It is lunchtime, sir,' Chandran said, looking around for a place to put the tray. Jha pointed him to a chair, and he kept the tray down and left.

In the evening, when Chandran came back with some cookies and tea, the lunch tray was still sitting on the chair, untouched. Jha was feverishly writing something on his papers, his frustrated state making it evident that he still had no answer.

Chandran placed the tea and cookies on a side table and asked Jha if he needed anything else. Jha grunted a 'no' without so much as looking up.

Chandran went near the retired major and said, 'Sir, why don't you take a break and come watch some cricket with us? It'll refresh your mind. It's the final ten overs, and it's turned into a pretty interesting match. I'll take your tea and snacks there.'

Jha turned his head, looked at Chandran and kept staring absentmindedly at him for a few seconds. Then, he got up, picked up his cup of tea and started walking towards the TV room. Chandran smiled and followed him, with the plate of cookies.

Jha and the boys watched the final overs of the match together, and he actually felt better and refreshed. He even called up Atri and updated him about the lack of progress.

He came back to his workstation and stretched out in the chair, arms folded behind his head, and stared at the ceiling. He could still hear Gupta and Chandran arguing in the other room over the intricacies of a leg-before-wicket dismissal. Jha kept staring at nothing, thinking all the time about what approach he should take next. He picked up the code and was looking at it when he heard Chandran say, 'But sir, LB cannot be given if both feet are outside the crease.'

Gupta replied, 'No, no, no, it can be still given if the impact is in line with the stumps. In that case, the LB still stands.'

As Jha heard them, his eyes flitted to the letters 'LB' in the third line. He sat up with a jolt and repeated 'LB … LB …

Leg Before'. As he ran his finger on the text, he wondered, 'Is it possible this code is based on cricket?'

He did a quick scan and found he could find a few two-letter combinations which were short for cricketing terms—'TM' could be third man, 'DP' could be deep point, 'DC' could be deep cover. Jha was now a man possessed. He immediately googled fielding positions and a glossary of cricketing terms and started working on the combinations. All he had to do now was figure out which combination of letters stood for which letter in the English language—and that was something he was very good at. In the past, he had cracked codes in less than a couple of hours with just one vowel to start with.

Jha started writing down each two-letter combination separately, and kept checking the terms on his phone. It took him less than an hour to finally break the code. Once he got a hint, he was like a bloodhound. The code looked a bit like below:

A—BO—Bowler
B—BA—Batsman
C—KE—Keeper
D—TM—Third Man
E—FL—Fine Leg
F—SL—Slip
G—DS—Deep Square Leg
H—PO—Point
I—DP—Deep Point
J—EC—Extra Cover

K—CO—Cover
L—MO—Mid On
M—DC—Deep Cover
N—LO—Long Off
O—LN—Long On
P—HW—Hit Wicket
Q—MW—Mid-Wicket
R—DW—Deep Mid-Wicket
S—SG—Square Leg
T—FS—Forward Short Leg
U—LS—Leg Slip
V—BS—Backward Square Leg
W—NB—No Ball
X—WB—Wide Ball
Y—LB—Leg Before Wicket
Z—CB—Clean Bowled

Jha had indeed managed to clean bowl the Code Man, again. But who would've thought an innocent conversation between Gupta and Chandran about what constituted an LBW dismissal would help him crack a huge, sinister plan in Kashmir?

As Jha completed working on solving the code, he realized that it was the address of four locations:

1. Old Radio Station

2. Girls Govt School, Paul Mohalla

3. Shaheen Carpet Factory, Shunglipura

4. Parvez Wood Works, Tarazi Khurd

The other two entries were 'GATE1' and 'GATE2', with the '1120' and '1125' next to them being timestamps.

Jha quickly opened the map of Srinagar and found all the locations within the city limits. Were these hideouts or possible sites for attacks? He did not have enough info yet to conclude that, but whatever it was, this was an extremely well-coordinated plan where the left hand didn't know what the right hand was doing. He realized that only someone who knew the whole picture could be moving the pawns. He immediately called Atri and asked him to come there ASAP.

Atri arrived in some time and Jha gave him the entire download, and even how his argumentative men had been critical to solving the puzzle. Atri hugged him and said, 'Sir, you are indeed the best. People have been working on this for days and you solved it within a few hours. Amazing, sir. Big respect.'

He saluted Jha very excitedly, and the senior man asked him to calm down. Atri proposed they go to Danny right away and discuss this in detail. Jha nodded, and as they were walking towards the door, Atri asked playfully, 'Sir, had these two not discussed LB and there wasn't a match going on, how long would you have taken to solve it?'

Jha smiled and said, 'You know, the last time I broke his code, he had used the initials of Bollywood stars, which I couldn't have guessed by any stretch of the imagination. I was struggling with it for a couple of days, but I happened to switch on the FM radio and the RJ kept praising Shah Rukh Khan and his movies and songs, calling him SRK again and again. And there it was—SRK—quietly hidden within a long incomprehensible sentence, right in front of me. The point is that hints are all around us, we just have to catch and understand them. So, to answer your question, I have no idea how long I would've taken had your boys not been discussing LB. Maybe I would've failed, maybe not. Who knows?'

Atri smiled back and they walked out of the house towards his Scorpio. 'We have a couple of hours before dark, sir. Let's get some recce done quickly and then meet Danny,' he said to Jha.

26

Sayema Haider was frantically pacing in her office in Srinagar, stopping occasionally to stare at the massive lake outside the huge glass window. She had sent an email to her ISI contact almost a week ago but had not heard back.

Finally, the day before, she had been intimated about the time for a phone call. Just half an hour ago, someone had come to her office, handed her a phone and asked her to throw it into the lake after the call. The phone had just one strange app installed, which was supposed to encrypt their conversation to counter any signal eavesdropping.

Sayema was still soaking in the beauty of the Dal Lake from her office, albeit irritably, when the phone in her hand rang. She picked it up even before a second ring. 'Hello?'

'Hello, Sayema, how are you doing?' came a cool, composed voice. This was her handler, Col Waseem Shah, one of the brightest the ISI had at its disposal. He was not one to be easily rattled; he knew what was going on and how Sayema's entire operation was on the brink of failure. But he knew that panicking alongside the panicky rarely led to any good.

'I am good, sir, but nothing is going as per plan. Bhat, whom the people your side fondly call "Code Man", and a couple of tracks were killed by the Indian Army and only a few have made it to Srinagar. I am not sure now how much the Indians know and what to do next. This is my first and most important operation. Please guide me on what to do,' she said, almost begging by the end.

'Are the brothers who have reached Srinagar enough to carry out the operation?' Waseem asked. 'Remember we had accounted for casualties and added more team members, so in the end, we should have enough numbers to do the deed. Doesn't matter who does it as long as it gets done. It takes only a couple to make it happen. As long as we have even one Ajmal Kasab alive, don't panic.'

His voice was still calm. As an experienced field commander and controller of many sources in India, Nepal and Afghanistan, he knew the best support you could give your team was patient listening and the promise of success. There's not enough money in the world to feed traitors anywhere; they always have some ideological or personal reason to choose this path. And that means keeping the fire alive. But once fear sets in—of failure or of getting caught—it was the job of professionals like Waseem to get them going and keep them motivated.

'Yes, sir, they are enough for now,' replied Sayema. 'But my main fear is what if the Indian Army and intelligence know about the plan and the locations of the explosives? Then everything will fail.'

She had taken this task more seriously than anything in the world. The ISI's contact in Srinagar had helped her secure the job of a communications consultant to the J&K chief minister's office. Now, she had the perfect access and location to carry out the ISI's bidding. She was hoping for a grand success in her first operation, and wanted the shining star status she was used to in the social media world.

Waseem let out a big sigh and said, 'Sayema, Sayema, don't worry. For every successful operation we carry out, at least a hundred fail. A single operation is not a benchmark of your capabilities or the reason for our success. Remember, bleed India with a thousand cuts! I am sure these guys will do the needful. But even if they don't, there is so much more to do. Have you forgotten our discussions? The Indian military is like a vicious watchdog. Sometimes we might get past, and sometimes we will get bitten. But our war is beyond this.'

He paused to let her digest this.

'The boss here is so impressed by the work you are doing in building narratives with your friends in the Indian media,' he continued. 'You have set social media on fire there with your connect. You targeted the government with those videos from Bangladesh that you passed off as "India", and before anyone could even post a rebuttal, your journalist and fact-checker friends had popularized them so much that they had billions of impressions and millions of comments, most of them abusing the Indian government. Don't think we don't notice these things. The work you are doing is phenomenal, and their clueless administration has no idea of how to deal with your brilliant strategy. Coming back to the plan, we have done all we could and put the wheels in motion. Now, we have to sit back and watch the chemicals react. Have some patience and confidence. We are working to bring India down; it will not happen overnight or with one attack or even a hundred. It will only happen by burning them in so many places and in so many ways that these tiny cracks give way to a final collapse.'

Sayema felt a little better after hearing Col Waseem's words. 'Thank you for your kind words, sir. I am doing my best here. I have even contacted the friendly human rights NGOs here and made contributions to them through our friends in London. Now, we all are eagerly waiting for their people to start writing and talking against India at all international forums. They are also planning to conduct debates and invite our friendly Indian politicians. The Western media loves when Indian leaders abuse India abroad. Within India, you know better than me that we have many media and celebrities on our side who will continue building our narratives and speaking against the government. I was just about to lose my head over the losses we are facing in this operation. But you said it right—as long as we have a few guys out there, this can still happen. I am grateful you took the time to talk to me. I really needed some motivation,' she admitted.

Waseem laughed. 'You are part of the team, young lady. We always look out for each other. Just drop me a message if you ever need to talk and I will get back to you. For now, just wait and watch. And let's pray all goes as planned. We'll have a party for you in Dubai if this goes well.'

Sayema got really excited at hearing this and thanked him again. She had never thought these so-called 'dreaded' ISI people could be so friendly and nice. She wished him luck and disconnected the call. Smiling, she got out of her office to take a walk next to the Dal Lake. And dispose of the mobile phone.

* * *

Col Waseem kept his phone down and turned a grim face towards the other officer who had been listening to the conversation through his headphones.

'So, what do you think?' he asked.

The other officer, Maj Shoaib Cheema, picked up his pack of cigarettes and put it at the centre of the table. 'Sir, you've placed her right in the centre, just like this pack, and made her think she is the boss of this operation. She has no idea about the code, she did not select the team, the target, the locations or the tactics. She is not even in touch with the guys. All she gets are updates from Frodo and Gandalf and reports to us. Yet, you are making her think she is controlling some big operation. I am not sure what you are prepping her for, but I can see it's a good plan. And she seems to be falling for it,' he said, raising one eyebrow and flashing a knowing smile.

Waseem smiled back. 'She's a narcissistic bitch who has been lying for years about her love for Kashmir and her thief of a father. We make sure she does what is expected of her, which I am told she is good at, and after that, I know for a fact that she'll crown herself as the queen of this operation just because we gave her the decryption key, which is not the right one, by the way. Only Frodo and Gandalf have the right one. They are both trusted and old-time assets.. As far as she is concerned, I'm sure she'll set the internet on fire through her contacts and that's what she's good at. So we make her think that she is bigger than what she is, ensuring that she does better than what she can do. Once and if the tables are turned, let her burn. Always, always keep sources like these on the fine line between acceptance and rejection. They'll keep struggling to prove themselves, and thus perform better. Never let them rest. When they Mess up, say "Don't worry". When they perform, tell them how close they came to ruining it. Got it?' the senior officer asked.

'Yes, sir, agreed sir, totally agreed,' Shoaib replied as they started walking out of the colonel's office. 'But I must tell you, I always laugh when I hear Frodo and Gandalf. What made you choose these code names for them?'

Waseem chuckled and said, 'Haven't you seen them? One is short, the other tall--they look like Frodo and Gandalf.'

They both laughed as they walked towards their car.

27

It was after dinner and Danny was playing a game on his phone when Atri entered with Maj Jha. Danny quickly sat up and greeted his friend, who then introduced the senior man.

Danny gave Jha a sitting salute by stretching his arms to his knees and nodding. Jha came up and hugged him and said, 'Heard so much about you, Danny. So glad to finally meet you.'

'The pleasure is all mine sir. I cannot thank you enough for coming here and helping us out,' said Danny.

'Anything, buddy, anything for the Army,' Jha said, parking himself in a chair.

Atri walked towards Danny and handed over a sheet of paper. 'As promised, here is the decoded document.'

Danny grabbed it eagerly and started reading. Then he looked at Atri and Jha, pointed at the paper and said, 'Explosives locations. Airport?'

Jha was so stunned he clapped softly. 'Brilliant, Danny, brilliant. No wonder you can sense bad guys moving in the jungle so precisely.'

Danny smiled. 'Thanks, sir, but there is no date mentioned.'

'I think we have a fair idea what is happening here,' Jha said calmly to both. 'The meeting was called by the ISI in Muzaffarabad to discuss the plan with Code Man, who was one of their most trusted guys. Around twenty to thirty terrorists were briefed by the same ISI team and they entered India from various points, heading towards Srinagar.'

He turned to Atri and added, 'And as you tell me, one track was killed in Baramulla and another in Kupwara by Danny's team.'

'If they were briefed, why were they carrying the coded document?' Atri asked.

'Because they were not told what the operation was. They were told they were going on a special mission, and to meet someone in Srinagar who would decode it for them. The Code Man was not supposed to come to Srinagar. It was his bad luck he got caught by Danny. The operation is very sensitive and secretive, so they did not want to risk the information getting out if someone was caught on the way to Srinagar. You are being sent to fight, but when and where, you'll be told in Srinagar.'

Atri looked even more confused. 'Since only the ISI, Code Man and the contact in Srinagar knew the key to the code, these tracks would have to come to Srinagar to get briefed on the operation by the agent here. What would Code Man do?' he asked.

Jha looked at Danny and then back at Atri. 'That is one thing I am not sure of. If the coordinator is in Srinagar, and he's to break the code, where was Code Man supposed to go?'

Danny stood up excitedly and summed up what they knew. 'Very "need to know" operation, sir. Everyone knows only one part, so absolutely no chance of leakage. Code Man selects the gang, takes them to the ISI for training and briefing, creates the code. The key is sent to the coordinator in Srinagar. The terrorists will get their final briefing on what to do and where to go, here in Srinagar. Code Man was supposed to peel off at some point to manage … something else.'

Jha nodded. 'Makes sense. Secrecy level maximum—till the time their guy in Srinagar decrypts the message, no one knows what to do. But I shudder to even think where Code Man was headed and why.'

Atri looked at Danny and said, 'You bloody three-pointer non-techie foot-soldiering idiot. Since when did you become so smart?' Everyone laughed a little.

Then, Danny asked seriously, 'Did you guys get a chance to think about why they are in Srinagar?'

'Yes, we discussed this on our way,' Atri replied. 'This, obviously, is a plan to blow up Srinagar airport with vehicle IEDs driven by suicide bombers. The rest of the terrorist teams also attack the airport and kill as many uniformed personnel and civilians as possible. I am sure they will try and reach the Air Traffic Control and other offices and cause a lot of damage.'

Jha mulled over it. 'If I were planning this, I would plan it at a time when flights would have just landed and there would be a lot of commotion. The attack would cause further confusion. Plus, I can truly make it to the global headlines if I enter the planes. So, given the large number of terrorists involved, it is a very serious situation. As far as the date goes, we were reviewing the VIP movement log that Atri got, and we have the home minister visiting here next week. You think that is the date?'

Atri shook his head. 'I doubt that, sir. The security is beyond imagination when the HM visits. Roads are blocked, and there are thousands and thousands of troops lined on them. The HM comes in a military aircraft at the Air Force airport anyway. So, that does not make sense,' he pointed out.

Jha stood up and, pacing up and down the room, said, 'What can make sense is to carry out this attack before he lands, so his trip gets cancelled. It makes a big statement for separatists that they did not let the HM come here.'

Danny sat on the edge of his bed, thinking silently. 'You are right, sir. This is going down within the next few days. And if we don't stop it, who knows what fresh hell awaits Srinagar.'

'Danny, once the code was broken and the locations from this page were identified, my teams did some on-ground recce. Two of the locations are very old and dilapidated places, with no one living or managing them. Did you see the list?' Atri asked.

Danny picked up the document. 'Old Radio Station, Girls Government School in Paul Mohalla, Shaheen Carpet Factory in Shunglipura and Parvez Wood Works in Tarazi Khurd. Gate 1 and Gate 2, 1120 and 1125, respectively. The first four must be where they have placed explosives, and these gate numbers and times are when the attack needs to happen. But this can't be it, right? The fighting teams will require much more briefing,' he said.

'You are right,' said Jha. 'So, I guess our mystery man here in Srinagar is not just holding the decryption key but will also brief the teams. He is much more important than we thought—he could be the main guy planning all this, sitting here in Srinagar. But we have no way of knowing who he is.'

Atri sat down on Danny's bed, took the document from him and had a long look. 'Sir, I think we have what we need to stop this from happening. I feel we should apprise the Corps Commander immediately, tear apart these locations, find the explosives. And do it all secretly. I do not suggest sharing this with civil administration because we have no idea who the mystery man is. And for someone to organize an operation of this size, I think he must be high up in the chain, and hence, the ISI's main guy here,' he said.

Jha nodded. 'If we had not broken the code, finding the mystery man would have been the top priority. But now, we can focus on finding the explosives and taking out any bad guys we find there. I know they are there!'

Danny stood up. 'I'm ready, let's go kill those bastards.'

Atri kept a hand on his shoulder and said, 'Calm down, Quick Gun Murugan! Let's talk to General Balhara first and see how he wants to take this ahead.'

Danny sat back down and looked seriously at Atri. 'Whatever the decision, I want to be part of it. You cannot leave me out, got it? I'll have my team here by noon tomorrow.'

Atri laughed and hugged him. Then, he held him by the shoulders at arm's length. 'That's why I love you, man. Till the time there are crazy gunslingers like you in the Army, nothing can happen to India,' he said.

Danny was in an excited and lethal state—lethal for the terrorists, that is. All he could think about was how soon he could get to those locations, and he was hoping the groups would be there for him to hunt down.

Atri turned to Jha. 'Right, sir. I think we should all get some rest now and put our heads together again tomorrow, and let's pick it up from there,' he said.

Jha nodded and was about to get up when Danny spoke up, 'Sir, if you don't mind, can I ask you something?'

Jha paused, looked at Danny, smiled, waved for him to 'go ahead' and sat back down. 'Why did you leave the Army, sir? You were the best intelligence operator the MI had in the Valley. People have difficulty believing the stories of your operations. You were decorated three times; your career was going great and then suddenly, you just vanished from the scene. Why become such a recluse?'

Atri and Jha could actually feel the pain in Danny's voice.

Jha had a serious expression by the time Danny finished. He kept his elbows on his knees and was fidgeting with his fingers, but stayed silent. Then, he looked up with pain in his eyes, nodded a couple of times and said, 'You know, a lot of people ask me these questions. And I always wave them off by saying that I had medical issues. But you guys are like my brothers, so I'm going to be honest with you. The fact is, I could not tolerate the way things were, and even are, in the Army. And I love my Army way too much to start hating it. But it became a bad marriage, and I thought a divorce was the best option. Now, I have a nice little job as the manager of a tea estate, my children are happy, my wife is ecstatic that we are all living together, my mother takes her walks and is in good health, and I spend my days going around the tea gardens and later sipping tea while relishing the view of the beautiful valley in the evening. I don't want anything else. I'm content, at peace and love my life.'

'Fine, we all know what's wrong with the Army,' Danny began, getting hot under the collar. 'The organization can do much better with less sycophancy, better equipment, limited autocracy, etc. But if every good person decides to leave, who will serve? The Army will be left with a bunch of mediocre and underperforming self-declared champions of leadership and it'll just keep degrading more and more each day. Good or bad, it is our Army, and we need to serve it.'

Suddenly, he brought his voice back down and said to Jha, 'Just my opinion, sir. We all have our experiences that shape our decisions. I may be wrong, but that is how I feel. Bashing bureaucrats and politicians, blaming everything on them, is our lone course of action. But what exactly do we do to improve the situation? It is our house and we have to mend it. If everyone decides to leave, it will not get any better.'

Jha started to say something but Atri interjected. 'Sir, I'm sorry, if you are tired, we can have this discussion some other day. Danny has been spending his days lying in bed and ogling at nurses, so I don't think he understands that you've been on a long flight and have been working non-stop since,' he said, giving a death stare to Danny.

'No, no, it's totally okay. I know very well who Major Danny Deka is. If he is asking me something, I would love to reply,' Jha said calmly, and turned to Danny.

'You are right about the principle of commitment. You are also right about the range of experiences shaping decisions. But what you are missing out is the individuality of people. You may love to spend a night in an ambush, but I may not. You may enjoy golfing with the bosses, but I may not. You may look forward to growth and your next rank, but I may not. Technically, it is the same experience, but both of us will come out of it with different learnings and motivations. Army men are empathetically handicapped, especially when it comes to juniors and subordinates. We all think "if thousands have done it, why can't he?" The efforts you put in to go beyond what you are required to do are a bonus to the organization, but what it really wants is your conformist submission to perform as a robot and do your daily chores. And I ... hold on,' Jha said, and fished out a vape from his pocket and took a deep drag.

Blowing the smoke, he said, 'Don't worry. I know it's a hospital. It won't smell.' The vapours from the vape quickly dissipated into the air.

Danny asked sheepishly, 'Sir, may I?'

Jha laughed and, handing the vape to Danny, continued, 'I gave it all I had, Danny. Day or night, awake or sleeping, my only thought was how to destroy the terror networks in the Valley. I submitted solid reports with proof about how some politicians, policemen and civilian office holders are OGWs and enablers. You know what happened to those updates? Zilch, nada, sifar, zero! I risked my life almost every day running around deep in terrorist areas as an undercover civilian. I could not speak to my family for weeks. I was hardly in touch with anyone because I never wanted to carry any phone or paper that could prove my connection back home or to the Army if I was caught. If I died—and thankfully I didn't—the organization maybe wouldn't have come to know for days. But, and a big but, it never bothered me, because I chose to do it and loved doing it. I always felt I was born to serve my nation. But you know what, when the time came for the organization to help me, it pulled its hand back.'

Jha paused, then continued, 'My father was diagnosed with cancer and had only a few months left to live. I really wanted to be there for my parents' last marriage anniversary. But the bosses didn't approve my leave. "Come on, Jha, if we all start taking leave for parents' anniversaries, who would work?" they said. My mother was howling when I called to wish them. My father could barely speak. It was that day I asked the existential questions that every officer asks himself at some point, Who am I serving? What am I doing? Who has my back? As a junior officer, I spend all my energy and focus on my troops' welfare, but who is concerned about me?'

Jha's face was twisted in deep agony, and he took back the vape from Danny and took a long drag. He blew the heavy vapour towards the idle ceiling fan, as if trying to grant it life and motion. There was pin-drop silence in the room.

Jha handed the vape back to Danny and said, 'My father passed away after a few months. After his cremation, I told my mother and sister that I had done three years in Kashmir, and I was due for a peace posting. I was sure the Army would grant me my choice of posting as I had to take care of my mom and sister. So, I requested the MS for Pune, where my family was. I took leave and met the AMS and explained my case. He was all friendly and supportive, and promised me that he would help me. You know where they posted me? Pathankot. When I requested to appeal my case, I was told there was no vacancy in Pune, and that I had spent six months in Pune around two years earlier too. I argued that I had been sent on a course to Pune—the Army had decided that it wasn't like I had wanted to be there. I said my family needs me, so this time I am requesting you to send me to Pune. There is a goddamn Military Intelligence School there, a whole counter-intelligence unit, a massive command HQ, the NDA, the CME (College of Military Engineering) and this and that. Pune is full of military establishments. How difficult would it be to add one officer to this strength of thousands? But the Army said your sister is not a minor, so you don't have to take care of her. And since she is an adult, she can take care of your mother. I told them my sister is struggling with depression, my mother has chronic back ailments. They brushed it off saying everyone has problems at home. So, I had to join at Pathankot and my life was a living hell. My sister's situation got worse, and all my salary and savings went into her treatment because the Army doesn't treat adult siblings. My mother was not only emotionally unwell after my father's demise, and even her physical situation deteriorated. She had to be hospitalized regularly and I could not be there. Both of them had no one around to manage even day-to-day affairs. The boss in Pathankot had some serious vendetta against intelligence guys, so he would call me frequently to poke and insult me.'

He paused again. 'So, to sum up, I was fucked from all sides and totally dejected that there was no one to help me when I needed it most. It was then that I decided to quit the Army and settle down elsewhere, find some peace of mind and take care of my family. It took another two years for the resignation to be accepted, but I did it. Sometimes, serving the motherland is a luxury we cannot afford because mothers at home also need us,' Jha finished.

'Sorry to hear all this, sir,' said Danny, almost whispering.

'Oh, come on. What I was trying to explain is that if you are demotivated and demoralized, you will make a very bad soldier. Weapons and tanks are accessories; the real weapon is the man inside. At some point, I realized I had no will to work and deliver results. I was not the man I had been—I was moving from one place to another like a zombie with no ambition or energy. My self-respect began nudging me. Is this how I wanted to wear my rank and uniform? Why was I fooling the system by just being a number in the parade-state? I was hardly productive, and on top of that, I realized that I had started to become very cynical and negative about the Army. I did not want that. Everything that I was, that I am, is because of the Army. I owed so much to it that I could not turn my relationship with it into some transactional agreement. I had vowed to serve come hell or high water. And at that point, I was not motivated enough to do that. So, honestly, it was not my problems but what those problems had made me that pushed me to resign. As I said, I love my Army way too much to ever be a freeloader or parasite. Better to break it off and maintain the love than force yourself to continue and become a self-declared victim who is always crying and whining,' Jha revealed.

'After I quit, I stayed in Pune for a couple of years. My sister got better, married and settled. My mom stays with me in Coonoor. I still love my Army as much as I did on the day of my commissioning, and I still get teary-eyed when I see Army movies and documentaries. But if it had to be unrequited love, so be it. It's like spending your whole life loving the most beautiful woman—like, let's say, what's her name … Kriti Sanon—and she never even knew you existed. I'm just happy about the fact that my love and dedication is true and unconditional, and whenever she needs me, I'll be there,' he finished, leaning back in his chair and smiling.

'Who, Kriti Sanon?' Atri asked.

'No, the country and the Army, you idiot. God, who made you a Major in Intelligence?' wondered Jha, shaking his head.

Danny continued to nod silently, and then said, 'I understand your point, sir. And as much as we have heard about you, I'm sure your words about your pain and suffering have barely scratched the surface of what you were going through. But I still have a question. If your dedication to the Army is so deep and unquestionable, irrespective of your resignation, why don't you serve the Army even now by being a voice that spreads positivity and motivation? I'm not able to buy the whole hermit makeover. Don't mind, but how can your confessions be valid if you do not back them up with actions? It just gives everyone a chance to presume and gossip the way they want. They don't remember Major Jha as someone who singlehandedly drove three terrorists as their driver to their destination and then killed them alone. Rather, the noise is that you were caught doing something unofficial and illegal, and were asked to quit rather than face a court-martial. On top of that, we have some cartoons from the MI masquerading as genius spymasters in the media, and people end up believing their made-up stories. The Army, needs people like you to come out with the real stuff.'

'That's exactly the reason I don't interact with anyone, Danny. I just do not want to explain myself and justify my actions. People who know me don't doubt me. And people who don't know me will never believe me, so what is the point? I cannot suffer fools and lose my hard-earned peace of mind by becoming some cowboy with claims, anecdotes and "strategic analysis" on TV channels. Millions have served in intelligence organizations across the world. Do you see them coming out and boasting about what they did? That is the single most defining characteristic of a true intelligence operator—learn to keep shut. If it is the media glare and public adulation you are looking for, you were a joker in service and a clown in retirement. The organization knows it, the professionals know it and most of the world also knows it. If some low-IQ, gullible crowd chants your name, that speaks more about you than them, as this is the level you can muster up as your "followers",' Jha said, using air quotes to stress his point. 'Since I was a famous guy because of my operations, a couple of channels did reach out to me for TV debates. I even went to a few. But the generals told the channels they were not comfortable with such a junior officer on the panel. The problem was that I wasn't all about the "when I was commanding so and so" generic anecdotal bullshit, and nor was I trying to please any government for a governor's post or a ticket in the next elections. I was calling a spade a spade, as ugly and broken as it might be. But, no one took kindly to my presence. It was shocking to everyone that someone would actually talk about what was wrong with the organization and how it could be mended. And mind you, I was not even a general who actually could have done all that during his command and service, but rather someone who chose to only speak about it after I retired. So, the calls from the channels died down and I was not too keen to pursue them either. I do write once in a while, but that's about it. Maybe someday I will write a book. Let's see,' said Jha, seemingly in better spirits.

It was nearly four in the morning.

Danny sat up straight and said, 'Sir, I cannot say I subscribe to your policy totally. But what I can say is that very few men have the courage to do the operations that you did, and even fewer walk away from all the pride and privileges success brings to just follow their principles. You put two officers together and the whining will start. And here you are, wronged and out of the system, and yet your love for the Army is unquestionable and unmatched. I can only say it is an honour to meet you, and if a time comes that I have to take such hard decisions in life, I hope I will have the courage and willpower for them. Thank you, sir, for sharing your story with us.'

Danny gave a two-finger salute and smiled.

Jha got up, hugged Danny, patted his head and said warmly, 'You are a legend, Danny boy. And meeting you was a great pleasure and honour too. It is always great to hug a brave and humble kid brother who is such a hero. Now you take care, get some rest and let's meet at 1100 hours to dissect this operation further. Shall we move?' Jha turned to Atri.

They said their goodbyes and Danny slumped back on his bed, wondering how difficult it must have been for someone to leave the thing he loved most. He realized he did not have it in him to quit the forces, no matter what. But then, as Jha said, we are all different—how we see life, how we react to it and what we expect from it is so unique. It would be foolish and naïve to expect the same outcomes for everyone in any given situation.

'Yeah sure, ask the chaps who get into encounters with me. They surely have different outcomes,' Danny said to himself, smiling, before he went to sleep.

28

anny called up Col Deo at 5 a.m. the next day and told him everything about the code and the plan. Deo was shocked to hear it.

Danny told him that Maj Atri had shared this information with the Corps Commander, who then wanted to meet them. Deo realized that maybe the Corps Commander wanted them to take on this operation, even though it was not their area. So, he told Danny he would start for Srinagar right away and would be there by noon. Danny requested him to bring Deepak and his Delta Company, Ghatak with him, along with his own QRT. Deo understood what Danny was hinting at, and the moment he kept the phone down, he passed orders for all the mentioned parties to be ready to move to Srinagar. He added a few more just to be safe.

They left Panzgam by 8 a.m. and reached Srinagar around noon, going straight to Corps HQ. Deo and Deepak reached Balhara's office to find Danny and Atri already waiting there. They exchanged pleasantries and asked the ADC to inform the boss that they had arrived. He returned with a message that they would have to wait till Brig Singh and Maj Gen Piyush Trivedi arrived.

They sat in the waiting room and Deepak asked Danny who Gen Trivedi was. 'He is the chief of staff at the Corps HQ. Although an Artillery guy, he is famous for an operation with RR, where he covertly planned a meeting with five area commanders of terrorists, and then killed them all in that meeting. The guy is pretty hardcore and understands CI very well,' Danny replied.

Deo was talking to Atri to understand more about the operation, when the ADC came in and said, 'Sir, he's ready to meet you.'

They went in to the Corps Commander's office one by one, saluted everyone inside and stood in a line. Gen Balhara and Gen Piyush Trivedi were sitting on the sofa and talking seriously, while Brig Singh was talking on the phone with his usual monosyllabic responses.

Gen Balhara got up and shook hands with everyone and asked them to find chairs. He then asked Atri to brief everyone.

Atri gave a detailed account of how they'd found the information they had gathered, and how there was a strong chance the locations mentioned on the page were the hideouts where explosives were being stored. Although two tracks had been neutralized, there was a strong chance that other groups had reached these locations and were camping there.

Balhara looked around the room and said, 'Gentlemen, first thing, all the people who know about this are in this room and I would like to keep it like that. And that means you too, Texan. Don't go blabbering to your girlfriend that you are Rambo part two of Srinagar.'

Everyone else grinned, but Deepak's face got red. People from Rohtak are called Texans in the Army, and as much as he was proud of that nickname, he knew this time it didn't come as a compliment. 'No, sir, I do not have a girlfriend,' he said.

'So, if you had one, you would've told her?' asked Gen Trivedi, mockingly.

'No, sir, of course not,' Deepak said, feeling trapped. Everyone was smiling. Deepak's face was burning. 'How do I become the target every time these seniors get together?' he thought to himself.

Balhara stood up. 'Fine, jokes apart, we have a very serious situation here. I'll tell you why I do not want to share it with the police and the local administration. First, we do not know how many of them are compromised. Second, they tend to leak such inputs to the press too. It will be chaos here if the media gets wind of some terrorists hiding in Srinagar with tons of explosives just before the HM's visit. It will alert the terrorists too, and we will have no way to trace them after that,' he said.

'So how do you plan to tackle it, sir? We are really short on time,' said Brig Singh, taking a seat.

'I think I will place my faith in the Gorkhas here and go for a small team operation at all locations. As I see it, if we can neutralize the terrorists before the city wakes up, it'll be a phenomenal success. But if we fail, I'll be hanged first. So, the question is, should I do what I think is right, or not, for fear of failure?'

Trivedi laughed. 'And you really think we don't know what you will do, Balhara?'

Trivedi was actually senior to Balhara, but had missed his promotion to Lt General. This was a rare but not unheard-of situation where the COS was senior to the Corps Commander. At such high levels, it all boils down to the chemistry between the generals, and Army HQ took the call to post these two stalwarts together because not only did they share an excellent rapport but they were also perfectly aligned as far as the Line of Ops went. So, while Trivedi was Balhara's junior in appointment, in the Army, once a senior, always a senior.

Balhara looked at Trivedi and just nodded. 'Sir, you always catch me. So, here is the plan. I want Danny and Deepak to take one team each and clear out these hideouts if there is anyone there. Their recent operations give me no reason to doubt their skills and capabilities. If not, we just grab the explosives and get back. The local Sikh unit will be available for transport and reinforcements, but they do not know what's going on. They will only step in if things get heavy for you boys. Deo, you and Atri will stay here at the HQ and manage control and communications. Can we do this?'

Everyone nearly shouted, 'Yes, sir!'

But Singh stood up and asked, 'Sir, why not call the SF (Special Forces) teams and get this done?'

Before Balhara could answer, Danny stood up and said, 'No, sir. Absolutely not!'

Everyone was shocked at the way this Major was behaving in the presence of two generals and a brigadier. Danny was seething when he said, 'Sir, what is it that the SF can do and we cannot? We have more kills in the field and fewer casualties. We generated this intelligence and we cracked this case. Every time there is precise and hard intelligence, the HQs always share it with the SF guys and send them ahead. Infantry units work much harder and do fantastic operations. This is not fair. While I cannot change how the Army operates, I can surely put my foot down for this operation. I assure you of success. We will capture all those explosives. Have some faith in us, sir.'

There was pin-drop silence in the room. Nobody knew what to say after Danny's stun grenade.

Finally, Balhara walked up to Danny and said, 'You'll go, don't worry. But what happened, did some SF guy steal your candy?'

Danny relaxed a little and replied, 'No, sir, nothing personal. I just don't like this favouritism and pampering. When it comes to acting on hard intel, I feel the RR and infantry units often miss out even after having enough experience and capabilities. Maybe commanders don't want to take chances, so they call the SF guys. And I agree, they are our finest. But that doesn't mean we should not be given a chance. Apologies, sir, if I overstepped.'

'No, no, buddy. Rarely do officers speak up. And it should be an eye-opener for old-timers like us. No harm, no foul. Let's work on the operational plan. But I forgot to ask, are you even fit to do this operation? I know you are walking fine but this might be a lot of strain,' Balhara said, patting Danny's back.

Danny replied confidently, 'I am ten on ten, sir. I've rested and recovered well. You had told the hospital commandant to give me freedom to move around, and that was a big help. I am totally ready for this operation.'

'Good. That's great to hear. So, Atri, how many locations do we need to check, and have you recced any?' the commander asked.

Atri sprang to attention and said, 'Four locations in total, sir. Old Radio Station, Girls Government School in Paul Mohalla, Shaheen Carpet Factory in Shunglipura and Parvez Wood Works in Tarazi Khurd. I had sent teams to recce all these locations. But sir, surprisingly, the carpet factory and the wood works don't exist. All these locations are old and out of use, but at these two locations, there is not even a building anymore. The other two, the radio station and the girls' school, are deserted buildings, and we could not detect any movement. My guys didn't hang around long in case someone was monitoring from inside.'

Gen Trivedi spoke before anyone else. 'It's a trick, Atri,' he said. 'Adding two locations that do not exist must have involved a lot of on-ground reconnaissance by these guys. It's an exceptionally well-planned operation, no doubt. The two locations that don't exist … it means the coordinator here wants to add mystery even at the last step, in case this code gets broken. They think the forces will spend time monitoring these locations, and they'll keep someone on the lookout because it's easy to detect someone hanging around an empty space, rather than a busy road or locality. It is an early warning signal for them—brilliant, in a way. You did well to call your guys back. I guess we will find goodies at the other two locations. What are the chances there will be people there?'

'Sir, most probably these guys would have heard from the coordinator, the mastermind in Srinagar, by now and reached the location. Even they would want to hide asap away from the eyes of security forces. Or they still could be on the road. There is no guarantee. The only thing I am sure is that the handler here in Srinagar would have shared the hide-out locations by now. The final briefing and decryption key for time and location will be shared one day before the operation,' replied Atri.

'Good, then,' said Gen Balhara. 'Danny, you are getting your wish. Surprise and action. Deo, I do not want more than one platoon strength in each team. I do not want to alert anyone unnecessarily. Let people know once the fireworks start and hopefully finish in the next thirty minutes at max. Can we do it?'

Col Deo stood up. 'Of course, sir. You are placing a lot of faith in the unit, and we will not let you down. I will closely monitor the operation and keep you updated,' he said.

The Corps Commander looked at everyone. 'Well, gentlemen, that's it then. These two, Danny and Deepak, will lead two teams to these locations and retrieve the explosives. If they find anyone there, they can 72 them in any manner they want,' he said. 'I just want a quick operation. No casualties and absolute secrecy till the time it's over. Any questions, anyone?'

Everyone replied 'No, sir', and Deo, Danny, Atri and Deepak started to leave the room. Brig Singh asked them to gather in the waiting room for further briefing and discussion.

Once they had left, Brig Singh said, 'Sir, you are taking a big risk here, and I'm sure you know that. Moreover most of this Op. is based on guesswork. We still don't understand that if the handler had to give the location verbally, why did they add locations in the coded documents. Also, if the decryption key was given to decode locations, the second part in the coded document about airport gates and time is then already known to the groups. We are missing something big here.'

Trivedi stepped in, 'Singh, you are absolutely right. And yes, there is a gap in our info. But here's the thing ... there has to be someone else with just the decryption key and only the location part of the code which must have been given by the Srinagar handler. He is the one who would have passed the locations to the group without knowing the time and location. Now the groups or that location guy don't know about the "when and where" of the attack. Only the handler has the full code. There can be more people involved but only with specific information about their tasks. Hence, let's go with what we have. Maybe it will take some time to figure out why Kattappa was killed.'

Balhara went behind his desk and added, 'I agree with Trivedi sir here. There is a lot more to unearth but for now, Surinder, let the cubs hunt. If we don't let them do so, they will never become lions. This Army needs more and more lions every day. While you and I sit here and mark maps with coloured pens, these firebrands take on terrorists every day, relentlessly and fearlessly. I think if you find a fighter, give him more rings and arenas to fight in, help him become more skilled. That's how we will improve our efficiency. We can plan as much as we want, but in the end, someone has to run through those hails of bullets towards the enemy trench to win that war. Might as well make that person a confident and ferocious killer. But then, I might be wrong. In another twenty-four hours, max, we will know,' said the lieutenant general.

Singh nodded, saluted Balhara and Trivedi, and left the room.

Trivedi looked at Balhara and said, 'You always had bloody verbal diarrhoea. It was impossible to shut you up in the NDA too.'

They both laughed and reminisced over their days together in the NDA.

29

The day was about to end and the skyline of Srinagar was slowly changing from yellow to orange—Danny's favourite time to conduct operations.

Danny and his team left their vehicles around half a kilometre from the Old Radio Station, because if terrorists were camping inside, that would raise an alarm. His team proceeded down the street while hugging the walls on both sides, and then through narrow alleys.

Walking through built-up areas is not easy—apart from the danger of getting shot at, maintaining surprise is next to impossible. Anyone noticing you would raise an alarm, and soon enough, the whole neighbourhood or street would be buzzing with people shouting and alerting everyone else.

Thankfully, Danny and his team managed to reach the building without being detected. It was a long, single-storey building that ran parallel to the main road, and was surrounded by a high boundary wall. The main gate was partially open.

Danny placed one squad of two opposite the gate and two more men on the far ends of the boundary wall. He signalled the remaining six to follow him, and slowly started to make his way to the main building after quietly entering through the main gate. He had been exceptionally cautious and silent.

He didn't know, however, that the three terrorists inside had already noticed the team, and were planning to ambush them the moment they entered the corridor, inside the main building, through its single door.

Danny reached the door to the building, taking cover beside it, with a scout on the other side. They both counted to three on their fingers and threw grenades inside. They still did not know if there was someone inside or not, but Danny believed in caution before bravado. This small precaution ensured that his team was not walking into a narrow corridor with lead flying from the opposite side.

The corridor had rooms on both sides, and the moment the grenades were thrown in, the terrorists took cover inside one of the rooms towards the end of the corridor. This gave Danny and his team a chance to cover some distance, but within a second, they all saw silhouettes and guns at the far end of the corridor and jumped into the rooms for cover. Danny's team ran into the room that looked out on towards the main road, while the Major, who was in front of them, went the opposite way.

Now, Danny knew he was trapped here—he could neither get out into the corridor nor go back to the entrance. The terrorists were totally dominating the corridor with their brutal firing, so Danny decided to jump through the window into the backyard. He realized he was all alone outside the building now, and a fierce gunfight was raging inside. His boys were giving it back to the holed-up terrorists nice and proper, but it would be impossible for them to move up the corridor, given the sheer quantum of fire that was coming from there.

He quickly scanned the area and realized he was in some sort of dumping ground for the radio station—there were wire rolls, garbage and rotting furniture all around. The building extended ahead for a few more metres. He could see the windows to each room in a straight line.

Bingo! I can outflank those guys and take them from the windows, he thought. But he had no idea which exact room they were in, and popping his head up in the windows to look for crazy men with violent personalities and automatic weapons was the biggest risk he could take at this point. What if they were already positioned to cover the windows? He would be shot even before he could peep out.

Danny decided to get crafty. He counted twelve windows in a row, two to a room, meaning there were six rooms. He crawled away from the wall towards a large wooden cable roll and hid behind it. He tried to guess which room they were in, and judging by the initial fire that came towards his team in the corridor, it would be safe to assume they were in the rooms towards the end of it. He picked up his AK and aimed at the last window, around a hundred metres away. A quick two-round burst shattered the glass. Danny waited, but the rhythm of the gunfight didn't change. So, they were not in the last room. He fired into the next room. Still nothing. Then, he fired into the third room, and within seconds, a hail of bullets came flying from the window and hit the courtyard wall. There they are, Danny smiled to himself. But now, they also know there is someone outside. 'Cost of doing business,' he muttered.

He started crawling forward, staying behind cover. When he was around twenty metres from the window, he paused and took position behind an oil drum. He aimed at the window and kept staring at it through his rifle's sights. His logic was, if they knew someone was out there, they would surely send someone to check. All he needed was a glimpse of that guy, and he got it within five seconds. An AK was jutting out of the window, and within seconds, a bearded man hesitantly peeped from it. That is all Danny needed. A three-round burst from Danny and he was hit straight in the face, propelling him backwards into the room. The spray of blood on whatever was left of the window was a perfect giveaway that he was not getting up again, ever.

The building he was looking at was built like a rectangular box with a corridor in the middle and rows of rooms running on both sides parallelly. On one side, the windows opened towards the road, and on the other, they opened towards the garbage dump where Danny was. The terrorists were hiding in these rooms and the gunfire so far had proved they were on Danny's side of the building. The building had around fifteen to twenty feet of wild and untended grass around it, and the area was also surrounded by a nearly fifteen-feet perimeter wall. The perimeter wall could easily save anyone in those rooms from fire and observation from outside.

But sadly, nothing was there to protect them from Danny's wrath.

He crawled a few metres ahead, still behind the cover of the random objects strewn around, and got a little peek inside the room. There was no movement but the gunfire was echoing noisily. He was beating himself up for not having a grenade at that moment. 'There has to be a better way,' he kept thinking, his eyes peeled on the broken, bloodstained window.

The terrorists inside knew there was someone outside the window, so they could turn their attention to this side at any moment, and Danny did not have adequate cover for a sustained fight. If they hadn't started firing on this side yet, it meant they had their hands full pinning down his team, and were also cautious about not going to the windows and exposing themselves.

With his team stuck in the rooms, there was no going back to them. All he had was himself to clear the room. Since no help is coming, let's try it my way, he thought, and picked up an empty plastic bottle and some rags from the garbage. He crawled back to a place where there were empty oil drums. He started checking these and found a little kerosene oil at the bottom of each of them. It was not possible to pick them up and drain the oil, so he used a stick to dip the rags and then squeezed out the kerosene into the bottle. It took him around two minutes to fill the bottle. Then, he shoved the rags into its mouth, and now had a petrol bomb ready, albeit with kerosene as the main ingredient.

Armed with his incendiary weapon, Danny started to hop from cover to cover towards the target room. Once he was close to the window, he crawled cautiously, with his eyes fixed on the window for any movement. In one hand, he had his pistol ready, and in the other, the bottle. He knew he was taking a huge risk, and the plan might not work. But he could not think of anything better. He stopped a couple of feet short of the window, put his pistol back in its holster and took out his special brass-edition Zippo with a lion engraved on it. He rolled the wheel and the sparks produced a little flame. He looked at the window again and moved a couple of steps forward to position himself perfectly under the window. He lit the bottle and the moment the rags caught fire, he threw it inside the room with enough force to strike the opposite wall. Since the plastic bottle would not break, the impact would force the kerosene to gush out and the burning rags would ensure that a large part of the room was engulfed.

The moment the bottle hit the wall, he heard a big 'whoosh' and then loud screams from inside. The bomb had done its job. He brought his AK, which was dangling to his side with a modified sling on his shoulder, stood up like an arrow and looked inside the room. One guy was running out the door with his back on fire and another was patting the flames on his pants. The wall and part of the room on the corridor side were burning furiously. In that split second, Danny decided to go for the guy in the room and let out a healthy burst of AK bullets, which caught the firefighter in his chest, and the moment he was hit, he forgot about the flames. His hands went up to his chest, and with his dying vision, he looked hard at the man standing outside the window, the one who had just outsmarted him. The terrorist fell with a big thump, and all his clothes caught fire immediately. Danny heard some gunfire and a loud shout in Kashmiri, and realized that the other one running from this inferno, with his back on fire, had been serviced by his guys in the corridor.

Danny decided against entering the room and ran back to the main entrance. He waited and announced to his team that he was coming in. Once they had confirmed, Danny entered and saw the burning body of the third guy lying ahead in the corridor, face down. His team came out with smiles, hurrahs and fist-pumping. His JCO pushed a guy ahead and said, 'He shot the terrorist.' Danny gave the guy a big hug and a pat on the back, and then asked them to finish the search.

The team quickly scanned the building and reported 'all clear'. Once secure, they started searching the building for explosives and found a big wooden case covered in tarpaulin, hidden under an old, broken table underneath a flight of stairs. Everything looked so innocent that no one could have guessed there were a few hundred kilograms of TNT just sitting there. The team hauled the box outside and waited for the team from Corps HQ to arrive and take charge of the TNT. They had doused the fires and dragged all three terrorists' bodies into the courtyard—the stench of burning flesh made everyone's stomachs churn but they had to be moved. They searched them but could not find anything substantial. Danny knew he had removed at least one pin that was holding the plan together.

Danny called Col Deo and Gen Balhara to update them on the progress. Soon, reinforcements arrived, and once the formalities were over, Danny left with his team to the transit camp.

But just as he was leaving, his new radio guy gave him the handset and said, 'Tiger.'

Danny took it immediately, and when he had finished talking, he was furious. Col Deo had told him Deepak's team had spotted movement in the Girls Government School in Paul Mohalla, and it looked like there were more than ten terrorists inside. Deo wanted him to reinforce Deepak before he ran into trouble.

Danny looked at his driver and said, 'Towards location two, full speed.'

He turned back and started briefing his team, quickly telling them about the development, and asked his JCO to brief the team in the vehicle behind. Then, he called Atri and updated him about this development.

Time to finish this, Danny thought to himself, as his hands wrapped around his AK in a fierce grip.

30

Danny's team took less than half an hour to reach Deepak's location. Deepak was waiting around half a kilometre from the school, his team under cover behind some shops.

As Danny's vehicles closed in, the scout from Deepak's team flashed his muffled torch twice to indicate their location. Everyone dismounted and Danny and his team crouched before making their way to the shop indicated by the flash. He greeted Deepak and crouched behind a stack of small wooden boxes.

'Yes, junior, what's happening?' he asked, sitting on a wooden stump and waving to everyone else to sit down. Deepak dragged over a wooden box and sat down too.

'Sir, we went to check the school and noticed some movement inside. Dhan Bahadur and I went ahead and did some recce, and we saw around eight to ten men inside. No one came out, but the windows were open and they were moving around casually. These guys have taken up three rooms in a row, with doors and windows facing a playground. The playground has these classrooms on one side and the boundary wall and the main gate on the other. Fairly simple construction. The first room in the row is locked and seems like some kind of office—maybe the principal's office. At the other end are two tiny rooms, most probably toilets. The main gate is the only way in, and the boundary wall is around eight feet high. We scanned it from across the road, from the rooftop of a small shop. And also, sir, I did not see any guard or anything. I think they're intentionally not keeping anyone outside the rooms in order to avoid getting noticed,' Deepak briefed him.

Danny listened intently while drawing circles in the dirt with a small stick he had found on the ground. He looked up when Deepak finished and asked, 'Why didn't you fire three rocket rounds into those rooms and blow them away?'

Deepak was befuddled. He had not expected this would be an option Danny would expect him to exercise. He started to stammer and said, 'Sir … but sir … I didn't know I could do that. Also, there are houses behind the school. What of civilian casualties?'

Danny laughed. 'Oh, calm down, D-Cup! I was just pulling your leg. You are right. We do not use Mister Carl Gustaf in built-up areas unless absolutely necessary. And as of now, it isn't. We can take them out without blowing up the building,' he explained.

Everyone was smiling as Danny was done teasing Deepak.

Danny got up in a swift motion but signalled to everyone else to keep sitting. These moments were when he was at his best—planning the imminent disposal of terrorists with his team.

'How many men and support weapons do you have?' he asked Deepak.

'Sir, eighteen men, two LMGs, one RL (rocket launcher) and one sniper,' Deepak replied.

'That's excellent. We have all we need. I have around twelve men, one LMG and one RL. We have almost a platoon size, and if we plan well, those clowns will be dead before daybreak.'

Everyone agreed with a quick nod.

Danny started giving orders, pointing at each person he was assigning the duty to. 'Deepak, you will place your sniper team and RL team on the rooftop of the shop across the road—the same one you observed them from. Four guys gone. Jeevan saab will take three boys and an LMG and cover the gate from across the road. Four more gone. Your second LMG and two more guys will cover the playground from across the street, from some other rooftop. Let's hope they get a good line of fire from there. My JCO Lok Bahadur saab will take a team of three and place a stop way ahead on the road to catch any runners. Four more done. You, Deepak, will join me in clearing the building. Keep your radio chap with Jeevan saab, we will take my operator. All the remaining guys will be part of room-clearance parties. I'll brief them separately. Any doubts, anyone?'

Subedar Lok Bahadur raised his hand. 'Sir, who will fire first? Your team or the sniper?'

Danny sat back down and said, 'We will. If the sniper shoots first, he will take out only one guy and alert all the others, and it will be difficult for the team entering the compound. My team will go for first contact, then the sniper has a free hand. The LMG guy on the rooftop is for precaution only. He will not—and I repeat NOT—fire once the encounter starts, because it is very close quarters and I don't want any friendly fire casualties. It is essential that we attack all three rooms together, because if we don't coordinate, upon hearing the gun battle, they might get time to blow up the room with the explosives. They don't mind blowing themselves up to take us out, and the entire neighbourhood will blow up with them. So, we all go together.'

Everyone said 'Yes, sir', and then began murmuring among themselves to thrash out the finer details. Meanwhile, Danny lit a cigarette and called Deepak to his side. He looked at him seriously and said, 'Stay behind me, okay? I will lead, then my radio operator, then four more guys, and then you. Don't try and jump the line in your enthusiasm. It is very important that you have control of the middle party. We will have a JCO saab to manage the rear party. Clear?'

Deepak felt a little let down. He was hoping to be the first or second person to enter the compound, but he realized it was better not to argue, lest Danny ask him to sit with the stops outside.

Danny got up after finishing his cigarette, crushed the butt under his toe and looked at his men. At these moments, he always knew he was leading these men into the most dangerous situations. They would do what he said, sit where he told them to, fire when he asked them to, and never back off, whatever the danger might be. He never showed it, but deep inside, he always had a fear of failure. Yet, he never hesitated, second-guessed or doubted his team's capabilities. He believed that if you had faith in your men, they would deliver. Overcautious leaders never make good battle commanders, he was very confident about this.

'Gentlemen, we have nearly ten trained terrorists inside. Once the firing starts, they will soon realize they are trapped. And you all know what happens when they know they are trapped—they fight like maniacs and throw everything they have at us. This operation would be a lot simpler if they did not have a large cache of TNT sitting with them. Then, we could have just waited it out and shot them one by one, even if it took days.'

Danny paused. He was about to ask his men to embark on the most vicious operation of their lives to date.

'Time is of the essence. There are suicide bombers in this squad, and they have boxes full of TNT there. The moment they feel they are trapped, they will try and blow themselves up and take all of us and the neighbourhood with them. That is not how we want to kill them. We want to be silent, swift and lethal. That's the party tagline tonight. And absolutely no grenades. I don't want to blow up that TNT myself. Any doubts?'

He looked around at everyone for signs of hesitation but found none. Only steely resolve glistened in their eyes.

'No, sir!' said everyone in unison.

'Good, get going with your teams. Send the entry team to me, I'll brief them myself. Once in position, confirm it to my radio operator. And the last thing, the firing only starts once the entry team starts firing. Even if the sniper or the LMG has someone in view, you will wait for us. Good, get going now. Jai Mahakali.'

Deepak asked, 'Sir, shouldn't we all move together?'

Danny waited for everyone but Deepak to leave and then signalled him to sit down again on the wooden boxes. He sat next to him and said, 'Never forget your basic tactics. The teams that go first keep an eye on the terrorists and cover them with observation and fire. The stops block their escape routes. Once everyone is in place, then we move under this cover. Should they sense our movement, we at least have a sniper, LMGs and a few AKs to pin them down. If we all move in together and then get detected, we will be scrambling for cover and firing positions. One foot on the ground, always. You will save your boys' lives and your own. Killing terrorists is never as important as keeping your team secure. And never forgetting basics will always serve you well. Flamboyance has no place in combat.'

Deepak kept listening and nodding.

They spoke for another hour, during which Danny briefed the entry team as well. By then, all the other teams were at their locations and confirmed this on the radio. Now, Danny asked the remaining team to move.

They got into single-file formations, one behind the other on both sides of the road and started their slow and cautious movement towards the school building that was now a fort full of armed-to-the-teeth terrorists with enough explosives to blow up the neighbourhood. Danny knew this was one test he could not afford to fail—whatever happened, the terrorists should not get a chance to explode the TNT.

Danny's team reached the location within half an hour and checked with all the teams. He asked everyone to check their weapons—safety catch off—and get into their smaller teams. He was taking two boys with him to clear room number one. Deepak was to lead another team, and Havildar Vishnu a third. The teams would move ahead, get close to the rooms and clear them out as fast as possible. The remaining guys were to position themselves just across the playground within the school compound and ensure that no one broke out of one room and entered the others.

Danny did a final check with the team across the road from the school gate. Then, he led his team to the gate, peeped through it for some time but did not see any movement. If anyone from inside the rooms was observing the gate, Danny had no way of knowing it. He would be walking straight into an ambush. Logic dictated they would have someone on guard duty.

But this wasn't the first hideout Danny had entered. Over the years, he had figured out that a small bag with a few items could solve problems for him. He called it his 'Sanjeevani Kit' for its ability to save lives in many tricky and dangerous situations. It included a pair of high-powered binoculars, Handheld Thermal Imagers (HHTIs), trip wires, flares, a mega laser-pointer, syringes, morphine, a range-finder, a cell phone without a SIM card, super glue and a few other items that were not part of the regular military kit. His team always carried this Sanjeevani Kit.

This time, it was the HHTI that came to the rescue.

Danny took it out and started observing for any signs of movement within the room through the doors and windows, as it was pitch dark inside and he could not see anything normally. He continued observing for a few minutes. Nothing. He felt relaxed and gave the HHTI back to his boys, who shoved it back in the Sanjeevani Kit. It was not abnormal for terrorists to not have a guard because often, tired from long marches, they would consume some drugs and sleep peacefully for hours. It was called a hideout for a reason—the anonymity of the place was the biggest defence against any intruder. Lucky for Danny and his team, this looked like the case here too.

Danny moved through the gap in the gate very slowly without creaking it open, and immediately took position next to it, pointing his rifle towards the rooms across the playground. He signalled and his team started to pour into the school compound and take their positions. The covering teams placed themselves on the two corners across the rooms on the main gate side of the playground. Two assaulting teams, led by Deepak and Vishnu, lined up one behind the other in the corner where one cover team had taken position. Danny moved to the far end of the playground with his team and positioned himself next to the other cover team in this corner. He would be moving along the boundary wall towards the principal's office, while Deepak and Vishnu's teams would move towards the toilets.

31

Danny waited to see that everyone was in position. He knew he had a sniper and LMG team covering his back. It was time to just go ahead and make it happen!

He signalled to Deepak to move ahead, and as those two teams went towards the rooms, Danny started too. 'That's a lot of firepower in one small compound. Well, that's a lot of targets too!' he thought.

Within a minute, all three teams were on the classrooms' side of the compound, with Deepak and Vishnu's team huddling next to the toilets and Danny's at the principal's office. At that moment, around twenty very deadly men, equipped with lethal automatic weapons capable of spitting out hundreds of rounds per second, were aiming towards the doors and windows of those three rooms, both from inside and outside the school compound. And yet, Danny knew that a little delay, one miscalculation, could lead to a huge blast, which would be the last thing he, his team and hundreds of civilians living around the school would ever hear.

He muttered 'Jai Mahakali' again, made a sharp 'move ahead' signal with his right arm to Deepak and Vishnu and ran towards the first room. His team followed him, and on the other side, both teams sprang like lightning bolts. It was about to get very noisy, very bloody and very chaotic.

* * *

Deepak ran to the middle room and took position just outside the door, while one of his boys glued himself to the other side of the door. The other two rushed to the only window and hid under it on the outside. Vishnu's team carried out the same drill outside the other room. It took them less than five seconds to achieve this, but they made enough noise to startle the occupants inside. Now, they could hear some movement.

In the background, Deepak heard a long AK burst from Danny's side, and knew the boss had started the fireworks. He immediately peeped inside, with his rifle pointing directly in his line of sight, and saw a man getting ready to stand up with one hand on the ground and the other holding a weapon. He was right under the blackboard. Deepak pressed his trigger and saw the guy's legs flying out from under him; he fell straight on his face. The boys in the window had found their targets too behind the first row of desks, and their AKs jutting through the iron grille of the window were spewing fire on two skinny guys trying to get up from their makeshift beds.

Deepak's buddy in the door next to him had taken 'clearing the room' a little more seriously and was spraying the room with bullets like he was watering grass in a garden. Deepak could see the chips from the furniture flying all around, so he gave a jerk to his buddy's shoulder, and shouted, 'Hey! Hey! TNT!'

The guy stopped and said sheepishly, 'Sorry, sir, I got carried away.'

Deepak realized that his window team had also stopped. He looked but could not see any movement inside. He asked his buddy to cover him and entered the room. Three men lay in all sorts of unnatural postures, with blood everywhere. Deepak shot a single round into each guy's head, just to be sure. He was learning fast! He signalled to his buddy to come inside, and they started searching between rows of desks and chairs, not only for the TNT box but for anything worthwhile. All this happened within thirty seconds.

* * *

In the other room, things were moving very fast too. Vishnu took the door along with his buddy, and his two boys covered the window. They got their first guy very easily, as he was sleeping on the floor right in the middle. He must have been shot by almost everyone and had more bullet holes in him than a sieve. But there were three more guys sitting at the far end of the room. Maybe they had been chatting till now. They got enough reaction time to position themselves behind the desks and start firing back. The tiny classroom, which should have been filled with children's laughter and giggles, was instead filled with the explosive noises of AK fire and shouting from both sides. The terrorists knew they had no time left. Vishnu knew he was running out of time. Everyone was desperate and wanted to finish this ASAP.

Vishnu's mind was racing. He decided to try a high-risk trick that had served him well in the past—he took out a grenade, and without removing the pin, threw it at the blackboard. He also shouted, 'Grenade!'

The inactive grenade fell on the ground with its distinctive clatter, and the terrorists as well as the window team jumped or ducked for cover. Only Vishnu and his buddy knew the pin was still in, so they both walked in quickly and saw the three terrorists lying on the floor, face down, their arms covering their heads. The terrorists could never have imagined that at a time when everyone was supposed to run for cover to save themselves from the shrapnel, the Gorkhas would be calmly walking in on them.

Vishnu and his buddy raised their weapons to their shoulders and fired a few quick bursts. The guys on the ground did not even get a chance to remove their arms from their heads. Vishnu tapped one each in their skulls and signalled his team to move in. He picked up the grenade lying on the floor and looked at his buddy, and they both smiled at each other. They started the search while the window team came inside and took positions next to the door and window, facing outwards.

Danny had asked both Deepak and Vishnu to secure the rooms and take defensive positions inside once the rooms were clear. Their task now was to keep the place secure and be ready for any counter-attack. For now, they were focusing on searching for the TNT and keeping an eye on the compound for any surprises.

* * *

Danny looked into the room his team had targeted and saw a makeshift barricade of desks and chairs at the far end. He could sense movement behind the barricade, which was around shoulder height. He realized the operation was not going to be as quick as he wanted it to be. And the barricade was a sign that this was where the TNT was kept. He had to get this done within the next thirty seconds or the terrorists would have enough time to open the boxes and blow up the TNT. 'Think, think, think, Danny,' he pushed himself mentally.

He looked at the boys covering the window and gave a small whistle to get their attention. The moment they looked at him, he signalled he was going in and shouted, 'Tight cover.' He then looked at his buddy on the other side of the door, who nodded back.

Moving under cover is one of the most commonly practised tactics in any military move, right from two individuals to large military formations. One team fires to subdue the enemy, the other moves ahead. Then the team which has advanced fires to subdue the enemy, and the other moves. That is how a group of soldiers moves as a single unit, covering each other.

Danny had added a twist to the tactic with his team. They operated regularly and understood each other well, so when Danny said 'tight cover', it not only meant basic firing on the enemy to make them hide behind the barricade, but also meant letting off a mad barrage of bullets and ensuring they did not even think of lifting their heads for the next few seconds. All Danny needed was just five seconds.

The window team and Danny's buddy in the door stood straight and pressed their triggers till their magazines fell empty. A single magazine takes roughly three to four seconds to empty, but rather than firing all together, if they fired one by one, they could get longer fire dominance—around ten seconds. And that's precisely what they did. This brilliant coordination and synergy in Danny's team had been achieved through hours of his guidance and training. It was during moments like these that this training was worth its weight in gold.

As Danny's boys let loose a ruthless volley of bullets, that hit the wall above and the desks in front of the hiding terrorists, the room turned into a cataclysmic black hole that seemed to be engulfed in unimaginable noise, smoke, violence and lighting-speed metal. Under the canopy of bullets, Danny ran, crouched and finally went sliding through the room to the other end, took his position with his back against the barricade and facing his boys, who were firing far above him. He signalled to them to keep going, and they slipped on their next magazines in a well-coordinated move, never letting the pressure of incoming fire on the terrorists reduce. Danny started crawling towards the end of the barricade, where there was an opening to come in and get out. With bullets flying and cement from the walls and wood chips falling all around him, he was confident that his guys wouldn't lower their aim, so he moved ahead quickly and finally reached the opening, which was like a U-turn at the barricade. He knew he could not fire sporadically or he might hit the TNT box, if it was there. And there were three guys inside, armed and ready with their rifles. One glimpse of him or his rifle and they would open the floodgates of bullets on him. He had to be very quick, precise and careful.

Danny placed his rifle's barrel to his chin, got into a lying position and in a quick move, slid behind the barricade. In that millisecond, he saw a man crouching, holding his AK close to his body, looking up towards the edge of the barricade, and then shifting his eyes to Danny. For Danny, it seemed like all this was in slow motion. He saw the guy shout upon seeing him, starting to straighten his rifle and point towards Danny, and then, suddenly, falling backwards with the force of two 7.62-mm bullets entering his forehead.

Danny took out the first one within two seconds of getting into the barricade and then aimed at the two guys behind his first victim, who were beginning to stand up and aim at him. Danny let out a quick burst and got one guy directly in the chest—he was thrown back upon impact.

All this happened within five seconds of him entering the barricade, and he was still lying on the floor, aiming upwards. As he aimed his rifle at the third person, he suddenly noticed this was a woman. He was shocked and could not react for a moment. And in that fateful second, the woman fired her AK at him. Thankfully for Danny, the panic of the situation, his position and her inability to shoot properly ensured that her aim was absolutely atrocious, and the bullets went way above him. She could not handle the recoil. But at the same moment, she had become so focused on firing at Danny that she forgot she had to stay crouched behind the barricade. She stood up straight while firing and the moment she stood up, she was thrown backwards with her head exploding and brains and hair plastered all over the wall.

Danny smiled softly and thought, 'I love my sniper!'

All three terrorists were dead in under ten seconds and Danny could still hear his team unloading their magazines. He turned back and shouted at his team to stop. And they did. He also asked them to get inside and help with the search.

He was right, the TNT was in this room, in two large boxes behind the barricade. The team came in and started their search of the bodies and bags. Danny stepped out and went to both rooms to check with Deepak and Vishnu. Satisfied, he called his radio operator and spoke to his teams who were positioned all around the school and asked them to fall back. He gave a report to Corps HQ, his CO and even updated Atri. He asked for reinforcements, which were on standby not far away, to come and wrap up.

Within half an hour, Danny was looking at the sun rising in the orange sky above the silhouette of rooftops of Srinagar, riding in a Gypsy towards the 15 Corps HQ and still wondering who the woman behind the rifle had been.

32

Danny briefed Gen Balhara and a few other officers once he reached Corps HQ. The total body count and the size of the TNT cache had been calculated, and the PRO was preparing a brief. The Army chief and the defence minister in New Delhi had already sent their congratulations to Balhara for this splendid, sharp operation. Very soon, the details would hit the national media. It was one of the biggest and best operations in Kashmir since the start of terrorism.

After the briefing, Balhara called Col Deo, Danny, Atri and Deepak in for a cup of tea, with Singh and Trivedi present in the room. With only the four of them in the room, they had a much franker discussion.

'Sir, we still have not discovered who the coordinator in Srinagar is and we don't know who the second person calling the shots on location is. We also don't know where Code Man was headed. There is still something going on, and as of now, we have no clue. Although I have someone working on it, it may or may not bear fruit. We need to step up our efforts. This was not a normal IED plan. The person planning this had much more sinister designs and the ability to execute them,' said Atri.

'I agree, sir,' said Deo. 'Although we will go back to Kupwara, I am ready to provide resources for this hunt whenever you need.'

Gen Balhara nodded. 'Thanks, Deo. And yes, Atri, we need to make a team to hunt this person down—an unofficial team of you, Danny and Deepak—since you all have total insight into this,' the commander said. 'Danny and Deepak and their QRT can be based in Srinagar for some time under the pretext of training, and you guys report only to me. No one should know why you are here. Deo, can you spare them for some time?'

'Of course, sir. No problem at all. It will be our unit's honour to work directly with the GOC,' Deo replied happily.

'Great,' said Balhara, sounding more like a friend than their big boss. 'Atri, you figure out the admin requirements and let Singh know what all you need. Only me, Singh, Trivedi sir and you guys will be informed about your real task here. Anything I can help you guys with? Danny, Deepak, anything?'

Danny cleared his throat and said hesitantly, 'Sir, if you can talk to the commandant at the Base Hospital … I do not want to go on sick leave. I'm totally fit and fine. I'm needed here.'

Balhara smiled. 'Sure, I'll talk to him. Your medical formalities will be taken care of. And you, Deepak? Can I do anything for you, young man from the land of wrestlers?'

Deepak replied in the negative, but had a question, 'Sir, do we have a press briefing again this time?'

Everyone looked at Deepak, and none of them spoke for a few seconds. They seemed to be in disbelief that someone could be stupid enough to ask this. But Gen Balhara had got the point.

'Neha is not available in Srinagar right now, she is working on her project back in Delhi. But I think she will be very happy to hear about your exploits. Singh, can we send Deepak for three days' temporary duty to Delhi, to visit Army HQ and get an update on drone procurements by the Directorate? Since he operates on the ground, he can give some feedback and help them understand the requirements of troops. Is that okay, Deepak ji? You can meet the officers in HQ in the day, and in the evening, you can give your interview,' he said.

Everyone in the room was now smiling. They knew Gen Balhara was being magnanimous and giving Deepak three days' break to go and meet Neha. Singh and Deepak both said yes, with the former rolling his eyes and the latter beaming with joy.

The meeting concluded and everyone walked out. Col Deo left for Kupwara after talking to Danny and Deepak.

Atri took Danny aside and said, 'Khan left a message for me. Apparently, his sister, Dr Henna, has some very interesting inputs she wants to share. You get your rest, and let's meet them in a couple of days. The mastermind is still out there.'

Danny just nodded knowingly, hugged him and said goodbye. Atri left for his unit.

Deepak and Danny went to the hospital, since Danny was officially still admitted there. Once in his room, Danny got onto his bed and Deepak took a chair next to him. Neither spoke for a long time and kept staring outside the window.

Finally, Danny broke the silence and said, 'Use protection, okay?'

Deepak blushed hard. 'Sir, I … I didn't mean it like that.'

Danny got up and patted him on the shoulder. 'Good job, D-Cup. Proud of you. And so are your men!'

Deepak was about to reply when Capt Rupali entered the room. She almost came running in and hugged Danny. Deepak stood up from his chair, not understanding what was going on.

Still holding Danny's arm, Rupali said, 'I just heard about the operation you did. You are a national hero. I am so proud of you. And I am sorry for acting strange that night. I had no way of knowing what was going on. Can we be friends again?'

She extended her hand sheepishly.

Danny gave a warm smile and said, 'Of course. I was fighting terrorists, but at the back of my mind, I was worrying about you getting upset. That is one operation I have no idea how to carry out.'

They both laughed and shook hands.

Deepak kept looking at them, confused. Finally, Danny introduced him to her. Deepak saluted Rupali and shook her hand.

Danny and Rupali decided to meet in the evening, and she left. The next moment, Deepak asked, 'Sir, what is going on?'

Danny settled on the bed and said calmly, 'She is a friend, posted here. She treated me. That's about it.'

Deepak raised his eyebrow. 'That's about it? Friend?'

Danny looked him straight in the eye and replied coldly, 'Yes, friend. And I do not want to discuss this any further.'

Danny was hoping for a timid backing-down from Deepak. On the contrary, Deepak laughed loudly and said teasingly, 'Oh sir, please. Don't give me that look. We are a team now. I am not scared of you anymore. We are warriors from the Gorkha Garrison out on a mission here. We are exterminators. The secret weapon of the Army. The two deadly barrels. Partners and friends. Right, sir?' He just went on and on.

Danny listened to him without smiling for a while. Then he got up, held Deepak's arm, twisted it and, holding him in that grip, pushed him out of his room. Deepak kept laughing all the way.

Danny gave him a final push and said, 'Get lost, friend. And don't disturb me till I ask you to. Now, go get yourself and the team settled before you leave for your approved debauchery.'

Deepak was still laughing. He saluted Danny, and as he was about to leave, he came forward and hugged him. 'Thank you, sir. For everything.'

Danny hugged him back, and as they parted, slapped him lightly on the cheek and said, 'Take care, buddy, and stay safe.'

Deepak just nodded and left.

Danny came back in, sat down in a chair and said to himself, 'Bloody D-Cup. Solid chap. Solid indeed.'

He sat down in his chair and happily started humming the original Nepali version of 'Musu musu hasi'.

This was the most peaceful Danny had felt in a long time. He knew he had just opened a door to some hell, and while he could not see the devil, the devil could see him. He knew the mystery man, or woman, would not like this failure, and that someone who was capable of coordinating such a big operation would not give in so easily.

He knew he and Deepak would operate in Srinagar now. It was time to get to the dark dungeons of this mystery and solve it once and for all.

33

'Yes, sir, all are dead,' Sayema said softly into her satellite phone. She was going through a serious crisis after having heard the news of the Army's operation. The worst part was informing Brigadier Zakir Khan of the ISI.

They had taken months to plan this operation, imported explosives through Myanmar and Kupwara, all the way across India to Srinagar. They had created an excellent team of handlers with each controlling the specific part of their operation effectively. The level of secrecy was such that even the guys who were to carry out the operation did not know what they were being prepared for. And yet, it had all fallen apart.

It was heartbreaking for Sayema. She was looking at the television furiously as she finished the call, and listened to the press briefing by the commander of the 15 Corps.

'You will pay, you all will pay. I swear,' she repeated again and again, as she took another pill for her splitting headache.

Finally, she picked up her satellite phone again and dialled a number. Once she heard a 'hello' on the other end, she simply said, 'Srinagar is over. Redirect to Jammu.'

And she disconnected.

GLOSSARY

ADC: aide-de-camp; an officer tasked with assisting general officers, governors and the President during ceremonial events and in administrative activities

Admin patrols: any movement of vehicles or personnel for routine administrative functions

AMS: Additional Military Secretary, an officer of Major or Lt Colonel rank tasked with human resource management of officers. Officers selected for such appointments have a great service record

AMC: Army Medical Corps

AOR: Area of Responsibility

Ayo Gorkhali: part of the Gorkha Regiment war cry—Jai Mahakaali, Ayo Gorkhali. It literally translates to 'The Gorkhas have arrived'

Battalion: an army infantry unit of approximately 850 men, commanded by a Colonel.

Brigade HQ: Brigade Headquarters

Brigade: an army formation consisting of three battalions with other supporting Headquarters elements, commanded by a Brigadier.

CHM: Company Havildar Major; an appointment responsible for administrative, disciplinary and day-to-day management of an infantry company

CI operations: Counter-Insurgency operations

CIJW: Counter Insurgency and Jungle Warfare

Company: an army unit of approximately 120 men, commanded by a Major or Lt Colonel.

Cookhouse: the place where food is cooked and served in a military camp.

Corps HQ: Corps Headquarters; Corps is an army formation commanded by a Lieutenant General. It ideally consists of three divisions, each having three brigades

Corps zone: the area of responsibility of a Corps.

First Four Gorkha Rifles/ ¼ Gorkha Rifles: First Battalion of Fourth Gorkha Rifles regiment of Indian Army

Foresight (of a rifle): the front sight of a rifle. It is the sighting device located at the muzzle end of the barrel that aids in aiming the weapon

GD: General duty

Ghatak Platoon: the commando platoon battalion, and in some cases, company

GHQ: General Headquarters (of Pakistan Army)

HHTI: Handheld Thermal Imager

HM: Home Minister

IED: Improvised Explosive Device

INSAS: Indian Small Arms System rifle

ISI: Inter-Services Intelligence; the intelligence agency of Pakistan

Jai Mahakali: war cries of the Gorkhas

Jat Ram: a colloquial term to denote someone who belongs to the Jat community in Haryana

JCO: Junior Commissioned Officer

Khukri: a large, curved knife or weapon used by the soldiers of the Gorkha Regiment

LMG: Light Machine Gun

LO: Liaison Officer

MI: Military Intelligence

MPV: Mine Protected Vehicle

MS: Military Secretary

MT area: Military Transport area; the location in a unit's area where vehicles are parked and maintained

NCO: Non-Commissioned Officer; the ranks of Lance Naik, Naik and Havildar come under this category

NDA: National Defence Academy, which is located at Khadakwasla, Pune, India

OGW: Over-ground Workers

ONGC: Oil and Natural Gas Corporation

Party: a colloquial term for any group of vehicles and personnel that are out on any duty

Pill box: a fortified defensive emplacement

Platoon: a subunit of approximately thirty-two personnel commanded by a JCO. It consists of three sections of ten men each

Post protection: the defensive plan and layout for the defence of an army camp

Psy ops: Psychological operations

QRT: Quick Reaction Team; comprising soldiers, support weapons and modified vehicles

Quadcopters: drones with four rotary wings

RFPs: official Requests for Proposals

Safety catch (of a firearm): a mechanism that helps prevent the accidental discharge of a firearm, ensuring safer handling

Sitrep: short for 'situation report', a report on the current military situation or operations in a particular area

Spur: A finger leading up a hill or mountain

Stand-to: an activity when all persons of a unit are on alert in their defensive positions

Stop parties: a group of army personnel used to block a particular route of ingress or egress

Subaltern: a young officer; upto the rank of Captain

Tanzeems: a terrorist group

TNT: Trinitrotoluene; the explosive yield of TNT is considered to be the standard comparative convention of explosives

Transit camp: the Administrative Military Camps used as staging areas for the movement of military personnel. Troops going and coming back from leave or duties use it

Unit: A colloquial term used for any military organisation that has a specific role, task and purpose

ABOUT THE AUTHOR

Maj Manik M. Jolly (Retd), SM is a decorated veteran of the Gorkha Regiment and Military Intelligence. He has operated extensively in Kashmir in counterterrorist operations and also commanded an infantry company and counterintelligence detachments. He is also a defence and geopolitics expert and writes for many reputed publications.

Danny looked through the gap in the window and saw an unconscious Deepak tied to a chair. Danny's blood boiled and he clenched his AK tightly.

He looked behind at his team and signalled them to follow him. He was about to take a step when he saw a beautiful young woman enter the room with a few men holding some electronic equipment. He quickly signalled his team to pause.

Danny couldn't hear anything, but he could see her directing other guys to place the equipment everywhere in the room. He was trying to make sense of it when he noticed one of the tall men placing a black banner with Arabic writing on the wall behind Deepak. Two guys were setting up a camera at the other end of the room. The woman was standing at the centre and directing everyone. He noticed a satellite phone in her hand.

And suddenly it hit him about what was about to happen. They were going to behead Deepak ISIS-style! His entire body became rigid and he could feel the blood pumping through his veins. Even though time slowed down at that moment for him, he knew he had none to lose now. He quickly counted the people and the AKs in the room, and realized he'd be entering the mouth of the dragon. A small closed room, too many AKs—a sure-shot recipe for chaos, smoke and lead. This would require everything he had ever learnt and practiced.

But it had to be done. There was no turning back now. He ran his finger on the trigger slowly to prepare, took a long breath and turned back towards his team to signal them to move. It was now or never!

HarperCollins *Publishers* India

At HarperCollins India, we believe in telling the best stories and finding the widest readership for our books in every format possible. We started publishing in 1992; a great deal has changed since then, but what has remained constant is the passion with which our authors write their books, the love with which readers receive them, and the sheer joy and excitement that we as publishers feel in being a part of the publishing process.

Over the years, we've had the pleasure of publishing some of the finest writing from the subcontinent and around the world, including several award-winning titles and some of the biggest bestsellers in India's publishing history. But nothing has meant more to us than the fact that millions of people have read the books we published, and that somewhere, a book of ours might have made a difference.

As we look to the future, we go back to that one word— a word which has been a driving force for us all these years.

Read.

Harper
Collins

HARPER
FICTION

HARPER
NON-FICTION

HARPER
BUSINESS

HARPERCOLLINS
CHILDREN'S BOOKS

HARPER
DESIGN

Harper
Sport

HARPER
PERENNIAL

HARPER
VANTAGE

हार्पर
हिन्दी